The W...

SUSANNA CARR

Heartline
Books

Published by Heartline Books Limited in 2001

First published in the United Kingdom in 2001
by Heartline Books Limited.

Heartline Books Limited
PO Box 22598, London W8 7GB

Heartline Books Ltd. Reg No: 03986653

ISBN 1-903867-31-2

Styled by Oxford Designers & Illustrators

Printed and bound in Great Britain by
Cox & Wyman, Reading, Berkshire

SUSANNA CARR

Susanna Carr has read short contemporary romances since she was a schoolgirl. The heroines pursuing and getting the life they wanted intrigued her. Although romance novels were forbidden in her home, she usually took one from her twin sister's secret stash.

Susanna longed to be a romance writer, although her pursuit was slow. She was a secretary before returning to college to earn a degree in English Literature. In order to pay her student loans, she worked during the day as an analyst and wrote romantic stories at night. It took seven years and several manuscripts before she received her first acceptance.

When she isn't writing or reading a romance novel, Susanna spends her time with family and friends. She currently resides in the Seattle area. She hopes her stories will find their way onto readers' keeper shelves and into her twin sister's secret stash.

Heartline Books –
Romance at its best

To Jane Porter, Sinclair Sawhney and Jesse Petersen
for their generosity and encouragement.

chapter one

'I can do this, I can do this,' Jessica chanted under her breath as she made her way to the impressive stone cathedral. 'I can do this.' Her hands clenched into fists. 'I *must* do this.' Had anyone other than her sister asked for this favour, she would have refused and not looked back.

A large shadow loomed over Jessica's tense figure. 'Tracy,' the deep masculine voice murmured next to her ear. The soft Australian accent pricked at her skin. She shivered, not from the dreary Seattle June weather, but with apprehension.

Jessica's muscles stiffened as she inhaled a faint whiff of expensive cologne. Her instincts screamed at her to run from the cathedral steps and take cover. Instead, she harnessed all the courage she could find within herself and turned, her legs wobbling in her twin's navy shoes. She prayed she would be successful with the crazy masquerade, as she jutted out her chin with false bravado.

Her eyes clashed with the cold brown gaze of Devlin Hunter, her twin sister's arranged groom.

Jessica's breath caught in her tightening throat. Devlin's unnerving presence had had that effect on her since the first time she met him six weeks ago. Back then, she had the luxury of creating an excuse and walking away.

Her heart thudded painfully against her breastbone as she studied the man in front of her. She was vulnerable prey, trapped under his watchful brown eyes. Her courage faltered as he frowned.

Devlin Hunter towered over her. His lean, athletic body

was sheathed in an elegant grey suit. Despite his executive attire, Jessica sensed the man could hold his own in a street fight.

But Devlin wasn't a man who relied on force. He was much too clever, too controlled for that. And his iron discipline made him infinitely dangerous.

Even at social events, people kept an eye on Devlin. Some reasoned it was because of his sexy good looks. His coal-black wavy hair and bronze complexion turned many heads. Jessica kept an eye on him for other reasons – it had more to do with self-preservation instincts. Only a fool would turn his back on Devlin Hunter!

Devlin's mouth twisted with derision. 'Do I pass inspection?'

Jessica felt her neck heat with a blush that would zoom to her pale face any moment. She wanted to stammer out an apology for staring. But that wasn't what her twin sister Tracy would do.

Jessica looked at him as if he was an insect carcass on the heel of her shoe. 'Your appearance isn't important,' she drawled in her best Tracy impression. The bored tone sounded rough to her sensitive ears. 'All that matters is that you're here.'

'You're lucky I came. Wedding rehearsals are a waste of time.'

'I couldn't agree with you more.' She looked away, indicating the topic was closed. Not only was it a technique her identical twin used frequently, but also Jessica didn't want Devlin to look at her too closely. If he noticed anything unusual about her appearance, she was in big trouble.

She would have pivoted on her heel and walked away, but that was courting disaster. One false move in the unfamiliar heels and she would be kissing the pavement. Definitely not the image of cool, self-assured Tracy.

Her sister's shoes were already pinching her feet. She didn't understand why Tracy preferred the pointed-toe heels. The navy double-breasted dress suit wasn't much better. It was as comfortable as a straitjacket. And the tights! It had been a long time since Jessica had found an occasion to wear opaque ones. Now she remembered why! Her legs itched for freedom.

Jessica felt ridiculous. She craved for her faded baggy jeans and sweatshirts. Her hair was twisted tightly in a chignon. She wanted to pull it back in its customary loose plait. Even the faint covering of cosmetics bothered her. She was counting the minutes until she could wash off the gunk. How could her sister stand dressing like this?

Devlin's heated gaze leisurely travelled down the length of her body. Jessica silently suffered the onslaught. She gritted her teeth and willed her arms not to protectively wrap around her midriff. 'What are you staring at?'

'I'm picturing you as the blushing bride surrounded in white lace and orange blossoms.' His voice was suffused with sarcasm.

Jessica's blue eyes flashed. 'And I'm picturing you as...'

'Tracy!' Her mother waved for her to join the small gathering of women at the cathedral's top steps. Was it only Jessica who noticed the panic behind the gesture? 'Come and say hello to your cousins.'

'Duty calls.' Jessica gladly took the excuse to leave Devlin. The less time she had to spend with the man, the better. 'I'll see you at the altar.'

'I haven't met your cousins. You must introduce me.' Devlin cupped her elbow with his large, callused hand. The simple touch made her nerves go haywire. She instinctively jumped away.

Jessica frantically tried to conceal her mistake. She smoothed a hand over her already neatly confined hair.

'You'll have plenty of time this weekend. I'm sure you would rather discuss business with my stepfather.' Tilting her head, she indicated the small garden at the side of the cathedral where Barry Parks spoke to a group of men.

Devlin's mouth twisted as he observed the older man. His glittering eyes deadened for an instant. It was no surprise to Jessica that Devlin didn't like her stepfather. No one did, but only a few were willing to work with Barry Parks. She wondered why Devlin wanted to. Tracy could easily explain to her how a tycoon's mind worked...if she were here!

The Australian turned and looked directly into her eyes. A slight buzzing filled her ears. She couldn't handle this man giving her his undivided attention. It would only mean trouble.

'Tracy,' he murmured. 'I'm getting the feeling you don't want me around.'

Jessica flashed him a sticky sweet smile. 'What was your first clue?'

'The fact that you're pushing me onto your stepfather and you don't want to be around for the discussion.'

Jessica's eyes shuttered, hiding her dismay. *Stupid, stupid, stupid!* Less than five minutes in his company, and she'd made a big mistake.

The real Tracy was a vice president of the family company and always kept informed. In Tracy's eyes, a private meeting with Devlin and Barry would be equivalent to professional suicide.

How was she going to cover this mistake? She tried to remember Tracy's only piece of advice on Devlin. 'Oh, it's easy,' Tracy had said. 'Act like a witch. It's the only way to handle him.'

Act like a witch. Jessica cringed. The role did not come easy to her but she had to do it.

'You make it sound as if I'm insecure about my job.'

Jessica bestowed upon him a slightly incredulous look. 'Please, I insist.' She shooed him away, while hoping at the same time that he wouldn't call her bluff. 'Go and speak to Barry.' Jessica bit the inside of her mouth, preventing the immediate apology for her commanding tone.

Devlin's eyes narrowed a fraction. Jessica's legs felt boneless. Here she was trying to help Tracy and she was a millimetre away from destroying her sister.

'Thanks so much for your permission.' Devlin's cold, clipped tone could form icicles on his words. 'Perhaps another time. At the moment, it would be best to meet your relatives.' He grasped her arm firmly and they made their way to the cathedral doors.

I don't know if I can do this... Jessica instinctively searched for Tracy. Tracy, who clucked over her like a mother hen, who always managed to get them into some scrape but yanked them out by her quick mind and quicker tongue.

Realizing the futility of searching for her twin, Jessica tried to gain eye contact with her mother. Maybe she could give some sort of signal for help. *No.* Jessica's gaze skittered away from her mother, the silent plea was too tempting and far too dangerous. *I can do this. I have to do this. On my own.* The knowledge was frightening.

She'd never done anything so outrageous in her life. She was the quiet twin. The other twin. The *good* twin. While Tracy cooked up schemes and elaborate ruses during their youth, Jessica would be at her side pointing out all that could go wrong.

Like this sister switch. No matter how many times Tracy insisted a role reversal would be fun to try out at school and at home, Jessica always refused. She knew there was no way she could pull off an impersonation.

And, as far as she could tell, she'd been right all these

years. Jessica might know every little detail about her twin sister, but pretending to be her was a whole other matter. It was also far from fun. Stressful, more like it. Fine tremors shook her body and a droplet of sweat slid down her spine.

She wanted to run back to Tracy's car and lock the door good and tight. Have a slab of steel between her and her sister's fiancé. Then she could drive off and never lay eyes on the intimidating man ever again.

But that would ruin everything. Letting her sister down in that manner would be unforgivable. And she would waste the opportunity to prove she was capable of helping.

But she didn't have to help her sister by being in the constant proximity of Devlin Hunter. 'You can let go of my arm,' she told him coldly. 'You're wrinkling the sleeve.'

Devlin smiled at her. A smile reminiscent of the jungle cat at the Woodland Park Zoo. He ignored her words and escorted her to her relatives.

Jessica flogged her brain for an appropriately acid command. She didn't think Tracy would tolerate being manhandled. If only Tracy had given her more information…

Rolling her eyes, Jessica realized how ridiculous that sounded. If anyone knew Tracy, it was she. They had shared a life together until she went to college and Tracy worked at shattering Parks Software Systems' glass ceiling.

Since returning from college after graduating with a computer science degree, Jessica noticed some changes in her identical twin. Tracy had transformed into a hard-edged, aggressive businesswoman. This new Tracy was more difficult to predict, but Jessica was certain that the core elements were unaffected as they lay hidden under the rough exterior.

Jessica believed it would only be a matter of time before she could once again predict her sister's actions. Until then, she would just have to expect the unexpected. She certainly didn't predict Tracy barging into her bedroom yesterday with a plea for help.

'Jessie, I need a big favour,' her twin stated as she surged through the doorway. Her fire-engine red power suit and slick brunette chignon commanded notice, but her vibrant presence shrunk the room, forcing all eyes on her.

The announcement was enough to pull Jessica's attention away from her over-sized computer screen. Usually, she was so focused on writing computer code to the point where people considered her absent-minded or forgetful. Tracy seemed to cut through all that, probably because this was the first time she had ever asked for help.

'Sure,' Jessica said eagerly, rolling her chair away from the Queen Anne desk. 'What do you need?' She wasn't going to make a big deal out of it, even though it was a signal of a shift in their relationship. If Tracy was asking for a favour, she must realize the hard-earned maturity Jessica had assumed during her college years.

'Uh, you might want to wait until I ask the favour,' Tracy suggested with exasperation.

Jessica shrugged, noticing that Tracy still hadn't outgrown the need to guide and reprimand. 'What do you want?'

Tracy started pacing the floor, the clicking of her red heels muffled by the faded Oriental rug. She manoeuvred around the untouched moving boxes Jessica had tossed aside once she returned home. Jessica had no intention of getting comfortable in her old room. She never did find comfort in it. It was too elegant, too refined. For a moment, she missed her casual, bright and colourful dorm room. It was cramped and she had to share it with her roommate, but it was cosy and welcoming.

Tracy was having trouble in making her request. 'I wouldn't be asking you this, Jessie, but I'm desperate.'

'Thanks.' Jessica's mouth twisted ruefully as she leaned back in her chair. 'Glad to hear I'm the first you turn to.'

'Sorry.' Her lips tilted in a small smile. 'I'm really messing this up. I'm not comfortable asking for favours.'

Isn't that the truth, Jessica thought. Tracy had a strong independent streak. She didn't want assistance or owe anyone. But Tracy did believe in getting repaid for the favours she gave, especially in the professional arena.

Family, however, was a different matter. Tracy treated Jessica with another set of rules. Tracy didn't think her twin owed her anything. Jessica had a sneaky suspicion that the common belief was she was *incapable* of returning favours.

Tracy, on more than one occasion, had insisted it was her 'duty' to take care of her younger sister. The idea of being someone's 'duty' chafed at Jessica. But she was just being given the chance to prove otherwise. If she could start returning favours, she might be able to demonstrate her independence and reliability. Of course, it would never repay for all that Tracy did for her…

'What's the favour?' Jessica asked.

'Tonight, I'm taking a flight to New York. I've been in secret negotiations with the most sought-after computer programmer.' Tracy dragged her finger along the line of the cherry four-poster bed. 'He's designed a hot new product and he's ready to switch alliance with Parks.'

'Which programmer?' Jessica kept up-to-date about the computer industry world, although it was from the outside looking in. Still, she hadn't heard any rumours on her email lists about a dissatisfied computer genius. 'Anyone I know?'

Tracy nodded as she plucked the floral canopy drapes with idle fingers. 'You've heard of him. He's written some of the most influential code for the Internet. But I can't tell you who he is. Secrecy has been a big issue with him.'

Jessica frowned. 'Sounds fishy to me.'

Tracy sighed irritably as she pulled away from the bed. 'It's the way this business works.' Everyone knew Jessica couldn't grasp the basic facts of business.

'What's the big deal in hiring this guy? I mean, what's in it for you?'

'It would show that I'm just as good – if not better – than my counterparts,' she declared passionately. 'Everyone wants this guy, and I'm going to win him. Once I sign this programmer on with Parks, I'll earn some respect around there.'

Jessica nodded slowly, understanding how much respect in the family business meant to her sister. Tracy was almost obsessed with it. 'So, what's the favour? You want me to drive you to the airport?'

Tracy struggled not to grin. 'Not quite. Tomorrow is also my wedding rehearsal.' She nervously rubbed at one of her pearl earrings. 'I'm not going to make it back in time.'

'What?' Jessica squawked as she gripped the armrests of her chair. 'You can't miss the rehearsal!'

Tracy made a face. 'A wedding rehearsal is an idiotic concept. There's no reason to make a big production out of it. Or a wedding for that matter. Anyway, getting this contract from the programmer is more important.'

'To you.'

'To Parks Software Systems,' Tracy corrected.

'Isn't that the reason why you're marrying…Devlin Hunter?' She stumbled over the name as her chest contracted. 'For the good of the company?'

'Barry thinks that arranging a marriage between me and Devlin will improve the stockholder's confidence in the company. And it will, if you're looking for a short-term solution. But the programmer I'm about to snag will make Parks the leader in Internet software!'

'Does Barry agree with you?'

Tracy groaned dramatically. 'Haven't you been listening? I haven't told anyone about this. Definitely not Barry. One whisper about my plans and he would give the job and the credit to someone else. I've worked for months on this guy. No one is going to take this project away from me.'

'You haven't told Barry that you're not making it to the rehearsal? Are you crazy? They kind of need the bride to be there.'

'Yeah, I'm aware of that.' Tracy paused and fiddled with her earring again. 'I'm hoping you can take my place.'

Jessica's mouth sagged open. 'Take. Your. Place.' She hadn't heard that correctly.

Tracy rushed to explain. 'I can't let anyone know what I'm doing, and I can't postpone the wedding rehearsal.'

'Then postpone the meeting with the programmer,' Jessica suggested, watching Tracy closely. When did her sister's priorities get so scrambled?

'And let some head-hunter get their claws into him?' She slammed her fists onto her hips. 'No way!' Her eyes flared with anger at the possibility.

'Why can't he just fly over here?' There had to be some other way to satisfy both of Tracy's goals. A way that did not involve some dangerous game of dress-up!

'I wish he would. Normally, that's how recruitment works. But this guy is special, and he knows it. He's testing us to see if we're going to treat him right. Having the Vice President of Recruitment fly to New York is one way of showing how much we want him.'

Jessica may not know much about business, but her sister's procedures sounded very odd. 'Do you really want to hire a programmer with a *prima donna* attitude?'

'I don't care if he has a Napoleon complex. Once he signs the contract, he will be Human Resources' problem.' Tracy studied Jessica's face. 'It's really important to me to sign this guy.'

'I know.' Tracy had worked non-stop at her stepfather's company, trying to gain the elusive prize of respect with a good dollop of prestige on top. From the sounds of it, this was her best chance.

'Can you pretend to be me?' Tracy asked softly, downplaying the outrageous request. 'Just for a few hours?'

A few hours! Jessica's eyes widened at the under-statement. Those few hours just happened to be when Tracy was the main attraction.

Tracy continued. 'I'll explain to Mom what's going on. I have to, since she can tell us apart instantly.'

'What makes you think Mom will go along with this plan?' Jessica grappled with the possible excuse. If her mother was against it, the two of them could talk Tracy out of the ridiculous idea.

'If I can convince her to take part in the plan, will you? I'll make sure she takes care of you,' Tracy added in a wheedling tone.

Great. Tracy can't even trust me to do the job by myself. She thinks I need a babysitter. 'That won't be necessary.'

Shocked silence flooded the room. 'You won't do it?'

'I'll…' she swallowed hard, 'do it.' Jessica tried to put on a brave face as her stomach churned. 'After all, how difficult could it be?'

'Thanks!' Tracy was vibrant with leashed energy. 'Thanks so much.' She zigzagged past the cardboard boxes and headed for the door. 'I'll go and tell Mom now.'

'Uh, before you go,' Jessica said, feeling slightly dazed as she sagged into her chair. 'Is there anything I should know?'

Tracy's forehead crinkled. 'About what?'

'How to act with Devlin?' Jessica prompted. She wasn't sure about the relationship between Devlin and Tracy. She rarely saw them together and had no idea how they interacted at work. How did Tracy treat Devlin? She hoped the answer was along the lines of ignoring him.

'Devlin? Oh, it's easy. Act like a witch. It's the only way to handle him.'

Act like a witch...act like a witch. The instructions repeated in her mind now, but Jessica couldn't seem to put the action behind the words. She meekly allowed Devlin to escort her to her relatives, wishing he wasn't so close.

She knew if she tried to wrestle out of his hold, Devlin would be even more determined not to let go. Wondering how her twin would handle the situation, and realizing any of Tracy's responses would be anticipated, Jessica decided to do the reverse. She relaxed her arm as a sign of surrender. Just for a moment before pulling away.

To her surprise, the move worked. She took advantage of her freedom and stepped ahead of him. Trying not to appear rude, yet keeping her distance, Jessica rattled off the introductions of her cousins to Devlin.

Jessica hoped her chatty cousins would descend upon Devlin, overwhelming him with their friendly interest. She needed a moment or two to regroup and calm down. Jessica wouldn't mind a chance to hear a few words of encouragement from her mother, but there was always the risk of being overheard.

Just as she expected, her cousins flocked around Devlin like fluttering birds. Jessica stealthily moved to the side, preparing to slip out of the group when good manners allowed.

Devlin anticipated Jessica's plan. And obviously disagreed with it. He placed his large hand at the middle of her back. Her entire body clenched. The heat emanated from him like a branding rod. Jessica resolutely made a show of ignoring his touch, as liquid fire scorched her muscles.

She nodded and smiled as her cousins chattered excitedly about the upcoming wedding. Jessica had no idea what was actually said. Then she felt Devlin's hand slip. She blinked, startled, as he slowly slid his finger down to the small dip at her waist.

Jessica wanted to bolt. She focused on remaining aloof, vaguely listening as Devlin charmed her cousins. She shifted her back so his fingers barely brushed the fabric of her dress.

Devlin didn't allow her a fleeting moment of freedom. His hand drifted to the soft swell of her hip and Jessica's nerve-endings tingled with alarm. He was too close.

She held her breath as he curved his fingers around her pelvic bone, boldly claiming his territory. She felt vulnerable next to his broad shoulders and chest. Fragile. The man effectively surrounded her. He was everywhere – above, behind, around her. She couldn't escape.

Jessica wanted to fight her way out of his intimate cage but she stood passively by Devlin, her muscles shuddering with slipping control. The urge was strong to claw her way out with arms and legs flailing wildly. She suspected a bride, arranged or otherwise, didn't assault her groom in that manner. And she was unwilling to find Devlin's counter-attack.

A movement caught her eye as an older woman tried to shoulder her way through the circle of relatives. Jessica was grateful for any diversion.

'Jessie! It's good to see you.'

Jessica instinctively turned and was met by her Aunt Lucy's fierce hug. She took advantage of the excuse to pull away from Devlin's possessive touch and returned the older woman's embrace.

Panic shot through Jessica. Did her Aunt Lucy just call her Jessie? She tried to rewind her brain. Maybe she was wrong. Maybe Aunt Lucy said 'Tracy'. After all, only Tracy would dress this business-like.

'Lucy.' Jessica's mother's voice cut through her chaotic thoughts. 'This is Tracy.'

The panic transcended into pure fear as she realized her mistake.

'It is?' Aunt Lucy pulled away and stared deeply at Jessica's face. 'Well, so it is,' she replied hesitantly. 'My mistake.'

'It happens to me all the time, Aunt Lucy. It's gotten to the point that I even answer to Jessica's name,' Jessica improvised quietly. She wondered if her excuse sounded credible. She had a feeling it didn't.

Aunt Lucy nodded slowly with polite understanding. 'I know just what you mean. Your mother and I had the same problem, but that was when identical twins were very uncommon. And where is your other half? I haven't seen Jessie since her college graduation last month.'

Jessica's mother interrupted with the planned excuse. 'Jessica is at home with the flu.'

Jessica nodded in support of her mother's lie. Her mother appeared to be very adept with subterfuge. It didn't take any time for Tracy to convince her mother about the plan, making Jessica suspect that the two had discussed it beforehand. Whether or not they did, it still came as a shock that her mother accepted the idea. Lorraine Parks made the navigation of Seattle high society an art form. She approached weddings and funerals as battlefields. It was odd she supported Tracy's decision of missing the wedding rehearsal in favour of hiring an employee.

'Oh, no! Poor Jessie,' Aunt Lucy wailed with disappointment. 'I hope it's the twenty-four-hour kind.'

'I'm sure it is,' Jessica said with confidence. 'Jessie wouldn't miss my wedding for anything.' She stepped out of her aunt's embrace and bumped up against Devlin. It was like colliding into a wall of granite.

'Oh, uh, Aunt Lucy, allow me to introduce you to my, er, fiancé, Devlin Hunter.'

'It's a pleasure to meet you.' Devlin's voice was like velvet brushing against the cool air. He shook the woman's hand. 'I didn't realize twins run in the family.'

'Oh, yes,' Aunt Lucy replied. 'They run rampantly in our family tree. You'll find out soon enough.' She gave a sly wink.

A vivid blush bloomed on Jessica's pale face. The day was bad enough without any mention of having babies with Devlin. The thought twisted her insides. Jessica cast a quick glance at the man beside her. She wanted to let out an unladylike snort at his wicked smile.

'Excuse me, sir.' Devlin's assistant, Nicholas, appeared at his employer's side with a miniscule cellular phone in his hand. 'You have a business call. It's urgent.'

'Please excuse me,' he said to the group, brushing his knuckles down Jessica's vertebrae. Her overwrought nerves erupted like stabbing needles and Jessica glanced down at the concrete pavement. She knew her eyes were flashing fire. The seemingly loving caress wasn't for the benefit of onlookers. It was a reminder to Jessica of who was in charge.

She felt, rather than saw, Devlin walk away. It was like a mountain of contained power had suddenly disappeared. Jessica quietly exhaled, but she wasn't able to relax. Her spine still burned from his deceptively casual fingers.

Jessica wondered how she was going to get through the next few hours. Hopefully she wasn't required to touch, speak, or be anywhere near Devlin Hunter. She had a feeling her hopes would not be realized.

Devlin flipped his cellular phone closed. 'That explains the "why",' he murmured. He stared thoughtfully at the group of women on the cathedral steps.

Nicholas frowned. 'Pardon?'

He turned to the man next to him and handed over the slim phone. 'That was Rawlins.'

The assistant nodded as he pocketed the electronic device. Both he and Devlin had spent many weeks in delicate, secret negotiations with the elderly Parks' stockholder. 'Did he change his mind again?'

'No. He's firmly in our corner. He called because he thinks the Parks family is on to us.'

Nicholas shook his head at the idea. 'Impossible.'

Devlin paused. He didn't have to explain everything to Nicholas, but his assistant was the only person he could trust. 'Tracy Parks just left his home.' He paused again. Devlin was used to keeping his own counsel. 'She was trying to buy his stocks.'

The assistant let out an irritable sigh. 'The man is eccentric, but I never knew he was senile. I hope no one else knows he's losing his mind. That could cause problems for us.' His eyebrows knitted into a frown. 'You didn't tell him Tracy was here. Why?'

'I believe Rawlins.'

'He might have a different meaning of "just", but there is no way Tracy visited him today. Rawlins lives in New York, which is easily eight hours away by plane.'

'It was Tracy,' Devlin replied with quiet, unshakable confidence. 'Today. I'm sure of it.'

'Then, who is that?' He tilted his head, motioning at Devlin's fiancée.

Devlin turned his attention to the woman again. 'That is Jessica Parks pretending to be Tracy.'

Nicholas' head snapped and he stared at the slight woman. 'No. No Parks is that gutsy. That stupid.'

'Guess again.'

Nicholas couldn't accept the possibility. 'Maybe it was Jessica in New York. That makes more sense. There would be less chance of something going wrong.'

Devlin shook his head. 'The Parks, especially Barry Parks, wouldn't entrust Jessica with a business matter.'

'How do you know that this is Jessica?'

Devlin turned, flashing a devilish smile. 'For one thing, Tracy hates me. This woman is scared to death of me.'

Nicholas' mouth twisted knowingly. 'I'm sure you'll use it to your advantage.'

'Yes.' He had to scare her enough to confess the entire Parks' plan, but not so much that she'd faint dead away.

'You know,' Nicholas said, 'I believe you, Devlin, but do you have any proof?'

'I'll get the proof. Make no mistake of that. I'll get to the bottom of all of this by the end of the evening.'

This evening wouldn't be soon enough. He had too much riding on tomorrow. He didn't know what the Parks family was trying to pull, but their timing was totally inconvenient.

Did they find out how deep his interests were in the company? No, that couldn't be it. They wouldn't be going through the motions of the wedding preparations. They'd be running for cover.

His eyes flickered across Jessica. If he were in a charitable mood, he would admit her impersonation was good. She had perfected Tracy's gestures and stance. But her clipped words were edged with nervousness, not arrogance. Her eyes couldn't mimic Tracy's confidence and cynicism. This woman's eyes shimmered with vulnerability and innocence.

Devlin scoffed at the idea. Innocence? Jessica grew up in Barry Parks' house. No one could survive that many years with the man without getting dirty.

Of course, he forgot that bit of truth when he first saw Jessica. Six weeks ago, she stumbled into Barry's study where Devlin was on the phone. Her pure blue eyes knocked him sideways. His chest contracted as she looked at him through her lowered lashes. She stammered an apology before scampering out of the room.

At the time, he wanted to pull her back into the gloomy study. His motives were unclear. Devlin didn't want to unsheathe his claws at her. He didn't want to torment her like a lion would a housecat. To be truthful, he was captivated by her quiet fragility.

Devlin shook his head with self-disgust. He fell for the ruse. He thought she was as she appeared – a naïve innocent. Now he knew better. The evidence was right before him.

Jessica Parks was knee-deep in this deception. He didn't care why she had got involved. He would destroy her – with the same systematic efficiency he would use to destroy her relatives.

Yes, Devlin thought with grim satisfaction, *there will be hell to pay.*

His eyes squinted thoughtfully. 'Nicholas,' he murmured. 'Let's force their hand.'

He could feel his assistant's growing interest. The man enjoyed a good strategic warfare. 'What do you have in mind?'

'Call Rawlins. Have him dangle the possibility of switching alliances to Tracy.'

Nicholas frowned with disappointment. 'What good would that do?'

'It might get more information out of Tracy. More importantly, it will stall her departure.'

'She might still make her flight. Tracy can be very resourceful.'

'But we are better. I'm sure we can think of a few other roadblocks.'

'I know we can.' Nicholas' eyes lit with an unholy glow and his body thrummed with the challenge. 'Do you want her to miss the wedding?'

'I want to see the Parks sweat it out.' He wanted them to scurry around like rats as their plans shattered and crumbled. And when the dust had settled, Devlin wanted to be the only one standing. The true and rightful victor. And then, just for a brief moment, he would know what it was like to reside in a just world.

chapter two

'I, Je-Tracy Lynn, take,' Jessica looked into the arrogantly masculine face and stuttered, 'th-thee, Devlin Caleb, to be my lawful husband.'

'Nothing to be nervous about, dear,' the elderly minister murmured. 'Every couple worries they're going to trip over the vows when the big moment comes. Just relax.'

Jessica smiled weakly and concentrated on her next line. It was difficult with Devlin lightly holding her trembling fingers. His hands were big but lean. She felt the latent power lurking underneath his warm skin.

'To have and to hold,' she hurried along. Jessica wanted to get this part over with. She was such a fraud. God was going to strike her down for impersonating her sister and practicing vows she had no intention of keeping.

'For richer or poorer.' She tried to focus on a spot right next to Devlin's face. Her courage would crumble if she had to give eye contact.

'In sickness and in health.' Devlin tilted his head just an inch. His brown eyes ensnared hers. 'Till death do us part,' her voice trailed off huskily. She wouldn't mind death by lightning bolt at the moment.

'Very good,' the minister decided. 'Just try to project your voice a little more tomorrow so the guests in the back pew can hear.'

Jessica mutely nodded her understanding and the clergyman explained the next part of the ceremony. She waited impatiently for the minister to step away and confer with the organist. Once he did, she discreetly pulled her hands out of Devlin's grasp.

'Nervous?' Devlin taunted.

Jessica bristled. Tension emanated from the man standing next to her. A dark, menacing aura swirled around him. She felt tendrils of silent danger snaking out, capturing her within its suffocating coils.

'Of course not,' Jessica replied, as she studied the cold marble floor. 'Why would I be nervous?' She placed her hands behind her back and twisted her fingers fretfully. The pad of her thumb rubbed against the unfamiliar engagement ring.

The ring shrieked wealth. She wasn't sure how many carats were mounted in the diamond jewellery, but each one of them was a nuisance. The maddening ring knocked against everything hard and snagged on anything fragile. It was also cutting the circulation off in her finger.

'You're acting nervous,' Devlin decided. 'Edgy.'

Jessica scoffed at the head-on assessment. 'Hardly. More like distracted. I was dictating an office memo in my head at the time.'

She hoped that would silence him. No such luck. Her wounding comment made the corners of his mouth twitch with amusement. Deciding she didn't have any weapons to fight him, Jessica ignored Devlin and studied one of the cathedral's stained-glass windows. The fervent images set in cobalt and crimson did nothing to calm her frazzled nerves. She looked around the cathedral, feeling very small and defenceless.

The size of the building intimidated her, just like the man at her shoulder. The dome ceiling had an ornate, supreme beauty and the dim lighting only added shadows, casting a golden glow around the altar.

'Perhaps you're having second thoughts.'

Plenty of them! She turned her attention back at the man, projecting irritation. 'Second thoughts about what?'

'An arranged marriage. Some people find the mere suggestion barbaric.'

Jessica shrugged. 'I don't see what the big deal is. My mother and stepfather have an arranged marriage. It seems perfectly normal to me.'

Great, just add another lie to my sins. If the marriage between her mother and Barry was normal, she didn't want to have a husband of her own. Her parents' marriage was cold and brittle. They might live under one roof but, as far as she could tell, they led separate and unparalleled lives.

Devlin's head pulled back sharply. 'Barry arranged a marriage deal with your mother?'

Jessica gave him a sidelong glance. 'What's so strange about that? I can't imagine Barry being governed by passion and love. Unless it had to do with his business.'

'What could your mother have possibly brought to the marriage?' His eyes squinted, the fanned lines on his tanned face deepening.

Jessica bristled with offence. 'My mother may not have been an heiress, but she came from a very respectable local family.'

The explanation was not good enough for Devlin Hunter. 'She entered the agreement as a debt-ridden widow with twin girls. I can't imagine Barry seeing that as a plus.'

Jessica openly glared at Devlin. 'A woman's dowry doesn't necessarily require stocks and property. A name – if it's the right one – could be priceless to the groom.'

Devlin's eyes glittered wildly. 'True,' he murmured softly. 'So very true.'

Jessica's skin prickled. There was something going on that she didn't understand, and she had a feeling she didn't want to find out. 'What about your parents?' she asked, reluctant to speak about her mother. 'Did they have an arranged marriage?'

'No.' His answer was clipped and controlled. 'They did not have an arranged marriage.'

'Hmm.' So much for easing into a more comfortable topic. His parents probably had a bad union. 'So this marriage probably seems strange to you.'

'Not really,' he replied silkily. 'I've dealt with stranger business mergers.'

She paused thoughtfully. The arranged marriage was a strange merger for Devlin Hunter. Odder still, was his interest in Parks Software Systems.

Years ago, he had made millions starting up dot-com companies in Australia and cashing in at the right time. Devlin Hunter was a young, vibrant businessman who was considered a visionary in the industry. It was understandable why Barry wanted to keep Devlin attached to Parks.

After Barry's heart bypass earlier this year, the company's stocks dipped precariously. Parks Software Systems suddenly had to battle the image of their company as old, tired and weak. Devlin's involvement gave rebirth to the company.

But why was Devlin involved with Parks? It had to be more than money. There were better chances to make billions with other companies. What did he see Parks offering? She may never know the answer to that – Jessica didn't understand the mechanics of business.

Jessica took a quick peek at her borrowed watch. It's only been an hour! It felt like forever. How was she going to last the night?

Devlin watched Jessica suffer under the strain of her masquerade. Strangely, he found no joy in it. Not even a zing of triumph.

She kept making mistakes and he didn't point them out. He could have easily emphasised the small errors, like her flinching whenever he touched her. The real Tracy would push him away, telling him, in no uncertain terms, what to do with his hands.

The big mistakes Jessica made surprised him. She asked about him, not realizing that it may already have been discussed with his future wife. She didn't even realize she was treading in a dangerous zone. Didn't she know not to ask questions? Didn't her family prepare her for this task?

Or did Barry assume that she had gained the Parks' trait of duplicity merely by observation? Why didn't Jessica's stepfather teach her the basics in pulling off a stunt like this? No, that wouldn't be Barry's style. He would drop a dove into a nest of vipers and have the bird fend for herself.

Dove? Why did he think that? She may not be as untrustworthy as Tracy, but Jessica was not as innocent as she appeared. He had to remember that.

Devlin's nostrils flared with impatience. He wanted this over and done with. He needed to call on her mistakes and stomp on any flimsy excuses. He wanted to shake her until she revealed the extent of her deception.

Instead he waited, stalking his frightened prey, closing his net slowly. He thought she would have collapsed by now. Obviously, threads of steel held together her gossamer-thin courage.

In that case, he needed to increase the pressure and watch her snap. He would keep her off-balance with whatever means he had to hand. But first, he needed to get her away from her accomplices.

Jessica made the untimely mistake of looking into his eyes at that moment. He imagined his eyes were wintry, freezing out any kind emotion. She certainly shivered and looked away.

'Cold?' Devlin asked, stepping closer. She jumped back as if he had suggested he would share his body heat. Her nervous reaction spawned a wicked idea.

'Uh, no. Hungry, actually. I haven't had a bite to eat today.'

'No wonder you look like you're ready to faint.' Devlin gave a brief glance at his sleek, modern timepiece. 'Let's go.' He wrapped his fingers around her delicate wrist and escorted her down the altar steps.

She scurried to keep up with his long-legged stride. 'We can't go now!' Jessica hissed, her words barely heard above the buzzing murmurs of the guests. 'The rehearsal isn't finished.'

Was that the best excuse she could think of? Devlin looked over his shoulder at his assistant, who was also acting as Best Man. 'Nicholas, let Father Woods know that the rehearsal is over.'

'Devlin, I want to stay,' Jessica said forcefully. He ignored her and continued down the aisle. 'My mother and the wedding planner worked on this ceremony. I had nothing to do with it, but I want to know what's expected of me tomorrow.'

Devlin halted as they stepped out in the vestibule. He spun around. His dark eyes searched hers intently.

Was that what this was all about? Did Jessica and Tracy switch places with the intent of continuing this throughout the wedding? Did they want him to marry the wrong twin? But then, why would they show their hand so soon? Why didn't they wait for the switch until tomorrow?

The switch at the wedding would make the marriage invalid. The marriage license and the pre-nuptial agreement had Tracy's name on it. But the CEO agreement did not indicate which twin.

He had to marry one of the sisters and become a member

of the family to hold the CEO position. Once he gained that status, he automatically assumed a large share of stock. Not so much as to control Parks Software Systems, but Devlin was taking matters into his own hands to accomplish that.

Did they really think that marrying the wrong bride would prevent him from reaching his prize? Devlin swallowed a harsh, humourless laugh. It was a waste of their time, but it gave him all the ammunition he needed, with plenty to spare.

Jessica drew back, but his hand clamped her wrist with the pressure of a manacle. He pulled her closer until her breasts brushed his hard chest. Devlin ignored how his lungs clenched as her softness rubbed against his ribs.

'Are you really going through with the wedding?' he asked. The switch would change the procedure of his plans, but not the outcome. In fact, it might work to his advantage.

'Uh, yes,' Jessica answered, looking at him with uncertainty. 'Of course.'

Devlin's mouth twisted into a snarl. He didn't want to hear that answer. 'Fine.' He stepped back and pulled her toward his midnight-black sports car. The aggressive lines of the machine mirrored how he felt at the moment.

Jessica began to resist. She dug her heels into the pavement. He barely heard the scratching sound, too intent to leave.

'What part of "I want to stay" did you not understand?' Jessica asked waspishly as the heel of her shoe skipped against a piece of gravel. She tripped and hopped inelegantly.

'There's no reason to rehearse every meticulous detail of the wedding.' Devlin aimed his electronic key ring and disengaged his car alarm. 'I'm doing you a favour by getting us out early.'

'Remind me to thank you later,' she muttered with sharp

sarcasm. He wondered if she was still in her role or if Jessica was able to be sarcastic.

He stopped in front of his car and walked around the machine. When she broke away from his hold and rounded the hood of the car, he paused. *Another mistake. Only this time, no more reprieves.*

'What?' Jessica asked, her voice edged with weariness.

'This is a McLaren F1,' he prompted.

Jessica blankly stared at him.

'You have to sit on this side, remember? It has a centre driving wheel. That side,' he nodded in her direction, 'has the stick shift.'

Jessica's eyes rounded with panic. Devlin wondered how she would cover her mistake. He didn't think she could come up with a quick save.

'You know, I came with my mother.' Jessica motioned at the sand-coloured Mercedes. Devlin admired her strategy to completely disregard her mistake. 'Since I still need to talk over the wedding plans with Mom, I'll hitch a ride with her. I'll meet you at the restaurant, OK?'

He opened the car door with efficient movements. The door swung up like a wing of a falcon. 'No need.' He watched her, silently challenging her.

Jessica glanced back at the cathedral.

'Get in the car, Tracy.' His steely command made her flinch.

Jessica tilted her nose in the air and marched towards him. 'Don't take that tone of voice with me,' she replied.

Devlin didn't respond other than lifting a mocking brow. He assisted her into the low-slung machine with gentlemanly grace.

As Devlin pushed the door closed, Jessica hurriedly belted herself into the car. If there was a trick with the seat belt, she wanted it solved before Devlin saw her.

She clicked the seat belt together with shaky hands as Devlin folded his impressive height into the McLaren F1. He slid in behind the wheel, his leg brushing up against her. She scooted closer to the door, but there wasn't much room. Jessica crossed her legs tightly, trying to escape from Devlin's close proximity.

The car easily roared to life under Devlin's capable hands. He swerved the expensive machine out of the parking lot but didn't speak. He didn't play music. Jessica couldn't stand hearing only the engine and the doubts bouncing around in her mind.

She had a nagging sense that, somewhere in the course of the rehearsal, she had made a huge error in her masquerade. But when? If she knew, she would correct it. She closed her eyes tiredly. This was hopeless. She wanted to flee from the car, from Devlin, and hide until the night was over.

No, she couldn't hide. She refused to take the coward's way out – it would be the ultimate failure. She would stick it through. Even if Devlin confronted her with accusations, she would deny it until she was blue in the face. Even if he had proof. Even if Tracy was in the same room.

'Do you think your sister will be able to attend the wedding?'

Jessica's eyes widened slightly. *Oh, God. He had figured it out already!*

'Having the flu and all.'

I am so stupid, came the immediate afterthought. *He's asking about me. Asking about Jessica.*

This was all too confusing. Jessica rubbed her throbbing temple with a shaky hand. She couldn't let her guard down for one minute.

'Jessica should be fine. She wants to be at the wedding

and will show up, even if she's sick,' Jessica said carefully. 'After all, she is the Maid of Honour.'

'She must feel left out of the events.'

I hope he's not considering dropping by the house to visit the invalid! 'I don't think so. She's very much a homebody.'

He frowned, the brackets around his mouth becoming more pronounced. 'She doesn't care about missing all this?'

Jessica dragged her eyes away from his face and watched the quiet neighbourhood zip by. 'She would hate missing the ceremony, but not the hoopla surrounding it.' Jessica wished he would get off the topic about her. It was difficult to discuss herself in the third person.

'Your sister sounds very intriguing.' Devlin's comment was awarded by an incredulous look. 'I've been lax in not getting to know her.'

'I wouldn't worry about it,' Jessica said, hoping he wouldn't take up on the idea. 'It's not like you'll see her very often.'

'Why's that?'

'She's just using our parents' home as a stopping point.'

'Barry mentioned he had other plans for Jessica. He's working on an arranged marriage for her with one of his competitors.'

This was the first Jessica had heard about it! 'She won't do it,' she said softly, as she battled down the rise of nauseating fear. If that was what Barry wanted, he would stop at nothing to achieve his goals.

'Why not?' Devlin asked. 'Doesn't she think arranged marriages are normal?'

'Probably.' Jessica gripped her hands tighter. They felt cold and clammy. She didn't want to talk about her marriage in the works. 'I-I think Jessica will hold out for something more.' Like love, respect, and shared goals for the future. But Devlin wouldn't comprehend that.

'More?' Devlin sneered at the word. 'You mean, she believes in true love? She's in for a big disappointment.'

Cynic. Jessica chose not to get into an argument about the topic. It might even be considered bad form to discuss marital love with an arranged fiancé.

'Maybe she'll change her mind once she sees the two of us succeeding.'

Jessica smiled and refused to reply.

'After all, look at us. We didn't like each other on sight. Who could've predicted how great we got on in bed?'

Jessica gasped. *What?* Her mind grappled with this unexpected piece of information, while her body reacted as if it had been plunged into boiling water.

'Hmm?' Devlin shot a sideways glance at her. 'What did you say?'

Jessica swallowed nervously. 'I…uh, didn't say anything.'

Devlin and Tracy were lovers? How could this be possible? Why hadn't Tracy said anything?

Did Tracy think she wouldn't find out? Her sister certainly had the opportunity to mention it! Jessica wasn't exactly asking for details, but she would have liked to have had some preparation.

Why did Tracy hide the fact that she was intimate with Devlin? It didn't make sense. The two of them together didn't make sense.

What was she saying? Of course it made sense. They were engaged to be married. It was natural. Jessica realized she was being naïve.

But she had never considered Tracy making the relationship physical. Her twin sister was hardly the poster girl of sensuality. Devlin, on the other hand, was the opposite. He was sex personified. Even with her inexperience in such matters, Jessica was aware of his aggressive sexuality. Obviously, Tracy had succumbed to his brand of carnal magnetism.

Wait a minute, Jessica thought as her mind flittered from one aspect to another. Attraction and lust had nothing to do with it. Tracy didn't operate that way. She was marrying Devlin Hunter because she wanted to be the wife of Parks' future CEO. Tracy would have an intimate relationship with Devlin, if it had to do with business. Enjoyment had nothing to do with it.

Jessica nearly ejected from her seat when Devlin placed his hand on her knee. 'It's been too long since we've been together.' His thumb brushed against her skin before dipping to the back of her knee.

His touch left a tingling trail on her sensitive skin. 'Mmm.' Jessica's mind whirled as her heart jumped into her constricting throat.

'Let's ditch the dinner and go back to my house.' His husky voice was designed to make any woman capitulate.

Oh no! How could she respond to such a bold proposal? She couldn't misunderstand or ignore it. Jessica tried to maintain her composure as her eyes wildly searched the street. *Where was that blasted restaurant?*

'I'll turn around at the next light,' Devlin promised in a seductive growl. Jessica took that as a threat.

'We are not missing the dinner,' Jessica informed him. A vein pranced nervously against her throat. 'It's bad enough that we walked out on the rehearsal.'

'We would have a better time at my place.'

Depends on your definition of a 'good time'. His definition would cause her to drop to the floor with a heart attack. But she couldn't tell him that. Although, considering his huge ego, he probably would take that as a compliment about his virility.

She had to think of an excuse, but her mind was spinning

out of control. *Think, think! How would Tracy reject him? Aha! Work.*

'Devlin, you know my idea of a good time would be at the dinner. There are quite a few potential business contacts I want to explore.'

Devlin's brown eyes sparkled. 'I'm crushed.'

'Sure you are.'

He sighed good-naturedly. 'I expect you to make it up to me.'

'Will do. On our wedding night.' And maybe she'd tell her sister about this deal. Then again, maybe not. Let Tracy find out for herself!

'Good idea.' His smile widened like a huntsman who had just snagged his first kill. 'I'll hold you to it.'

'Of course it's a good idea. I thought of it, after all.' Jessica smiled back, the anxiety slowly seeping from her muscles.

She couldn't believe how easy it had been to get out of that sticky situation. Tracy's sexual relationship with Devlin must not be that passionate. Now, why did that make her feel better?

Devlin swung into the restaurant's parking lot. He quickly found a spot next to the building and parked his beloved car. 'It was a good idea,' he murmured as he turned off the ignition, 'but not good enough.'

'Huh?' Her eyes widened as he captured her hand and raised it to his mouth. She had just fallen for the oldest trick. The moment she had relaxed her guard, he had pounced. She was so mad at herself she could spit.

'I don't feel like waiting for our wedding night,' Devlin explained. He kissed her knuckles, then turned her hand over and placed a kiss on her palm.

Her lungs squeezed tight with alarm. 'Yes, you can. The anticipation just makes it sweeter.'

'You know anticipation doesn't turn me on. If I want something, I want it now.' The hot look he gave her made it clear that the 'something' he wanted now was his fiancée.

'B-but, the dinner…' she frantically glanced around the parking lot and looked for her guests.

'Surely you have the time to spare one kiss,' he said. He efficiently unsnapped her seat belt and pulled her close.

Jessica stared at Devlin as her composure fractured with anxiety. *What have I got myself into?*

chapter three

Devlin drew her closer. He didn't rush or grab. He didn't need to, since Jessica stared mesmerized at his masculine beauty.

His bronze skin glowed with health. She absently noted that his face was smooth and clean-shaven. The aggressive angles of his jaw indicated his determined, unyielding personality.

She fought the compelling need to reach out and trace the harsh outline of his face, before delving her fingers into his lustrous black hair. Sanity returned to her full force when her lips were just a kiss away from his mouth. *What am I thinking? This is my sister's fiancé! The man she's sleeping with!*

Jessica hastily turned her head just as Devlin's mouth brushed against her jaw line.

'Tease,' he whispered. His warm breath skittered across her flushed skin and blew against a wisp of her hair.

'It's bad luck to do this before the wedding,' Jessica improvised.

'Didn't stop us before,' Devlin growled, as he nibbled an ascending trail to the tender flesh below her ear.

'Uh, I mean the day before.'

'Strange superstition,' he grumbled against her skin. The low vibrations pulsed inside her. Her breath hitched in her throat as he nipped her bare earlobe.

'Nevertheless…' she weakly argued. Her eyelids drooped as her heart clattered against her breastbone.

Devlin's sensual quest halted. His mouth rested against

her ear. Their raspy breathing echoed in the small confines of the car.

Jessica found the quiet nerve-wracking. She hastened to break the threatening stillness. 'I'm a superstitious person,' Jessica said.

'Is that right?' Devlin pulled away.

Jessica took his retreat as a good sign. Would he respect her reasoning? 'Yes. Very superstitious.'

Devlin didn't appear to be listening. His hands softly cupped her face, his eyes intent on his exploration. He splayed his hands and tangled his fingers into her hair.

Delicious sensations danced across Jessica's shoulders and back. Devlin's blunt fingertips rubbed against her scalp. Jessica sank her teeth into her bottom lip to prevent a pleasurable sigh from escaping.

Devlin withdrew his hands and let them tumble against her ears. Jessica shivered when he caressed the outer curves. She pressed her face against his strong hand. To continue or stop his exploring, she wasn't sure.

'Tracy?'

Jessica frowned. *Tracy?* She flinched as her sister's name filtered inside her sluggish brain.

'Tracy?' Devlin asked again as Jessica pulled away from him. She ran a tense hand through her hair.

'We should go inside,' Jessica decided. She turned away from Devlin and studied the car door. She wondered how such a contraption opened. She would stare at every inch of the car if it meant not looking at its owner.

Jessica heard Devlin mutter a frustrated oath. He angrily pushed his winged door open and uncurled his lithe body from the machine. Jessica jumped as he slammed the door shut and strode around the car to assist her.

I can't believe I acted that way with Devlin. I wanted to touch him! I needed his touch. What is wrong with me? He's going to be my brother-in-law! Sour bile burned her stomach.

She wasn't going to touch him again. Even if her impersonation depended upon it. She would never forgive herself for coveting her sister's man.

The door next to her swung up. Jessica sharply turned her head toward the sudden movement. Devlin towered over her and extended his hand.

Jessica tried to ignore his assistance but the stubborn man took her resisting hand and helped her from the seat. Her hand tingled from the brief contact.

OK, this will be the last time I touch him. She dropped her hand from his and took a step to the side as he locked his car.

Devlin seemed oblivious to her body language. He placed his hand on the small of her back and escorted her to the restaurant's main doors. Jessica held her spine rigid.

Right. This will be the last time I touch him. She waited as he opened the door for her and she hurriedly walked inside. She tried to walk in front of Devlin, but he easily matched her steps and took hold of her elbow.

Jessica wanted to groan as her arm threatened to melt from his touch. She had a feeling it was going to be a long night.

Devlin kept an eye on Jessica throughout the rehearsal dinner. She tried so hard to avoid him without looking too obvious. If there wasn't so much at stake over the wedding, he may have found her attitude amusing.

He should tighten the net he cast around her, but the distance suited him for the moment. Let her worry and keep looking over her shoulder. She'd wear herself out before the night was through. And he could stand back and work on his next move. One that involved no touching. His pretence as the amorous fiancé may have knocked her off-balance, but it had also backfired on him.

His mind drifted back to their clinch in the car. He gritted his teeth at the memory and tried to focus on the physical evidence he had. Forget DNA or having Jessica trip over a web of lies. He could call off the wedding right now. All because of a missing pair of earrings.

Tracy had pierced ears. It was a fact many knew. He gave her Australian pearl earrings as an engagement present that she wore often. Not out of sentimentality, Devlin was sure, but because of the hefty price tag.

Jessica didn't have pierced ears. She'd never had them pierced. There were no marks or blemishes on her earlobes. If he confronted her on that, her courage would crack. If he compounded that piece of evidence along with the string of mistakes she made, Jessica would be on her knees confessing.

So why didn't he go in for the kill? True, it didn't go with his strategy, but he'd been known to improvise on a few occasions. But still, he hesitated.

He noted a movement at his side. Turning slightly, Devlin saw Barry striding toward Jessica. Nothing secretive or sly about Barry's manner. More like a showdown.

'Tracy,' Barry's voice carried an angry bite. 'A word with you.'

The chattering bridesmaids apparently heard the dangerously clipped words. They practically flew away from Jessica like frightened birds.

Devlin's curiosity peaked. Why did he call her Tracy? Was he worried about being overheard? If so, he wouldn't be confronting Jessica at the party.

He silently surveyed Barry Parks. The older man appeared as hard and as cold as his personality. The weathered, craggy face and white hair drew attention, but people took a second look at his glittery amber-coloured eyes.

Devlin then took a moment to observe Jessica. She kept her face blank as she met her stepfather's dark glare. The woman must have learned early on not to show any expression around Barry Parks. He would use them to his advantage.

Jessica straightened her shoulders as if preparing for battle. 'What is it, Barry?'

'Are you trying to sabotage this wedding?' he asked in his gravelly voice.

Her eyes momentarily widened with surprise, as if Barry was totally off the mark. 'I'm not doing anything to destroy the wedding,' Jessica declared calmly.

Barry's eyes squinted with disbelief. 'Then why did Hunter cut the rehearsal short and hustle you out of the church? And why did he look as mad as thunder when we got to the restaurant?'

'Why do you think?' Jessica countered.

Barry jabbed a bony finger at her. 'I think you are purposely causing trouble.'

Devlin silently whistled as he listened to the exchange. He couldn't believe it. Barry knew nothing about the sister switch.

Which meant he had no idea about Tracy's meeting with Rawlins.

That also meant that Jessica and Tracy were defying Barry. With the help of Lorraine, their mother. He flashed a brief glance at his future mother-in-law. The image of a lady. Her role was so perfected that no one saw the scheming manipulator lurking underneath. He had no doubt that she had a hand in the scheme.

Were they trying to destroy him and, inadvertently, Barry? Did Lorraine think he was usurping her daughters' places? He was more than willing to prove otherwise, but it wasn't the time or the place.

Or were they trying to oust Barry from his self-made throne? One he had built from crimes and double-crossing?

Devlin couldn't blame them, but it was a useless effort on their part. They were no match for Barry Parks.

And if they were trying to destroy both Barry and himself, they couldn't begin to contemplate their punishment. Because they would fail, Devlin was willing to bet all his money on it. And they would suffer.

Jessica most of all. His gaze flickered on her once more. Lorraine would sacrifice her daughter and cut a deal. Devlin's mouth twisted with distaste. He knew her type. Tracy would escape unscathed. She thought on her feet and would lay blame on the closest sitting duck. Which was Jessica. She had no weapons. Her allies would abandon her, which she probably wouldn't believe until it was too late.

He shouldn't care. Jessica was the opposition. An inferior, pathetic opposition, but the enemy just the same.

'And you better watch your mouth,' Barry continued to bluster. 'If this wedding falls through, I am holding you and your mother responsible.'

'Mom?' Jessica asked. 'Why would you blame Mom?'

Barry flashed her a shark-like smile. 'Because I can.'

Jessica glared at her stepfather with intense hatred. 'You are scum.'

Barry's face mottled and he took a step closer to his stepdaughter, effectively intimidating her. 'Don't you get sassy with me.'

Devlin had heard enough. He walked forward, deciding Jessica needed a little saving.

'You can't order me around anymore,' Jessica whispered hotly as she took a cautious step back. 'I'll be another man's property tomorrow.'

Devlin knew, without a doubt, that Tracy would never say such a thing. It seemed Jessica had trouble saying those words as well but, instinctively, he knew Barry would understand the idea.

The problem was that Devlin understood the idea all too well. He thought he was a civilised man, yet the idea of Jessica being 'his' slammed his stomach.

Barry laughed. 'Is that what you think? You'll still be under my influence.'

Jessica tilted her chin and bravely took a trembling step closer to her stepfather. 'Devlin isn't influenced by anyone,' Jessica announced. 'And he would have a problem with someone ordering around his wife.'

Devlin filed Jessica's statement in his mind. It seemed that she knew exactly what kind of man he was. She was more people-smart than he gave her credit. And his future father-in-law never recognized how dangerous Devlin could be. He would soon find out.

'Ha!' Barry said harshly. 'Devlin will thank me for keeping you in line.'

'No one needs to be kept in line,' Devlin smoothly interrupted the argument. Barry held his ground as Jessica skittered to the side. She looked like she wanted to make a run for it. Like she was being ganged up on. Devlin didn't like being lumped into the same category as Barry Parks.

He stealthily stepped next to Jessica and placed his arm around her shoulders. He tried to silently convey his possession to Barry without frightening Jessica. 'I could do without a scene at my wedding,' he told Barry wryly.

'Great,' Barry snorted. 'I'm getting a hoity-toity son-in-law.'

He knew Barry was trying to save face. The man valued prestige and high society more than he let on. 'If you will excuse us, Barry. I think Tracy has neglected the groom long enough.'

'By all means,' Barry agreed, gesturing with authority as

if he had a say in the matter. 'Take her home before she causes any more problems.'

'Goodnight, Barry.' Devlin firmly wrapped his hand around Jessica's arm and silently escorted her to safety.

It took a few moments for Jessica's racing heart to slow down. She never did well with confrontations, especially with Barry.

She absently grabbed the flute of champagne Devlin offered her. 'Thank you,' she murmured. She took a deep breath, wondering how much Devlin had heard of her discussion with Barry. 'And thank you for getting me away from Barry. He gets a little argumentative when he has had a lot to drink.'

'What was he arguing about?'

'He felt it necessary to lecture me on my behaviour,' Jessica answered carefully.

Devlin shrugged. 'You know parents. They can't break the habit of telling you what to do.'

His comment niggled an observation she had made earlier that evening. 'Speaking of parents, I noticed your parents didn't make it to the rehearsal. Will they attend the wedding?'

Devlin's handsome face darkened swiftly. His eyes clouded with malice as the skin tightened against his prominent cheekbones.

What have I said? Why did I make him angry? Maybe he has already discussed this with Tracy. I've messed up royally this time.

'My parents are unable to attend,' he replied abruptly. She sensed the control he used as he spoke. 'They convey their best wishes.'

The message was stilted. The tone was formal and aloof. 'Are they against this marriage?' Jessica ventured.

Devlin gave a harsh bark of humourless laughter. 'On the contrary, they support it wholeheartedly.'

'Oh.' Devlin didn't seem too thrilled about his parents' acceptance. This fiancé of Tracy's was difficult to understand.

A ghost of a smile lingered at his mouth. 'Our duty is done here. Let me take you home.' He placed his hand at her back once again and escorted her out of the function room.

Jessica's heart rate rocketed to top speed. Home? Which home? His or mine? Or does it make a difference to him as long as there's a bed?

The man was determined to get his fiancée into bed. Only this time, she was prepared. 'It sounds wonderful, but I can't.' Jessica hoped the disappointment she was projecting masked the relief she felt.

Devlin's eyebrow rose. 'Can't?'

Jessica allowed her footsteps to slow down to a shuffle. There was no way she could leave the building with Devlin. 'It's almost midnight,' she explained.

'And your fairy godmother's spell will be broken?'

Don't I wish! Jessica smiled. 'Our wedding day starts in five minutes. It's bad luck for the groom to see the bride on their wedding day.'

Jessica's body rejoiced with victory. Throughout the party, she had tried to develop complicated scenarios to excuse herself from any potential rendezvous with her sister's fiancé. In the end, her irrefutable reason was so simple.

'As you know,' Jessica continued, 'I'm very superstitious.'

'That's true,' Devlin nodded as he directed her to the pay-phone alcove. 'But we still have five minutes.'

'Wh-what?'

'And, as you know, we can accomplish a lot in five minutes.' His dark eyes twinkled wickedly.

'What? Here, in the restaurant!' She looked around the hallway but there weren't any people milling about. For now. 'Are you crazy?'

'Don't you remember telling me?' He backed her up with uncanny stealth until her shoe hit the wall. He bracketed her head with his forearms, effectively barricading her.

'Uh…no,' she whispered. Her heart pounded in her ears. Her stomach was freefalling.

'Of course not.' He leaned into her. She felt surrounded by his heat. 'You're forgetting everything these days, aren't you? Must be from wedding jitters.'

Jessica's tongue nervously darted across her parched lips. 'What am I forgetting?'

'You wanted me to fulfil your fantasies.'

'My fantasies?' she squawked, trying to ignore his belt buckle digging into her stomach. Her mind was exploding. She had to get away without making a scene. She had been so close in making this pretence successful.

Her brain tried to grab the first idea. None developed. Her body was reacting in a different matter. His body felt deliciously warm and she wanted to curl up against him.

'The fantasy about making love in public,' he reminded her huskily. 'You talk about it a lot.'

This is not happening! Jessica wanted to run, but her feet didn't move.

'I was joking,' she said, her voice cracking.

'No you weren't, and we both know it.' Devlin shook his head. 'You said you found the idea of getting caught so arousing. I'm making that fantasy into reality,' he promised, as his head swooped down to her bewildered face.

The moment his mouth touched hers, Jessica knew she couldn't handle the situation. She couldn't allow Devlin to kiss her. He was her sister's fiancé. It was wrong and dishonest.

On the other hand, she couldn't refuse Devlin. If she did, he would wonder why his formerly eager bride was suddenly unwilling. She didn't want him to suspect anything so close to the wedding.

Jessica tilted her face at an upward angle. Devlin placed slow, seductive kisses down the column of her throat. 'We really shouldn't do this,' she whispered roughly.

Devlin raised his head and met her bemused gaze. She found the twinkle in his eye confusing. 'Why not? We're going to be married tomorrow.'

No, we won't! her mind shrieked. She was about to say that their marital status didn't matter, but Devlin captured her mouth with his.

A savage wave crashed against her as he deepened the kiss. She moved her shaking arms from the wall and sought Devlin's solid chest. She needed to hold on to him lest the sensual storm swept her away.

Jessica returned his kisses mindlessly. She needed the intimate touch as much as she needed her next breath. She palmed the powerful chest and felt Devlin's pounding heartbeat.

Devlin speared his tongue between her lips and explored the moist cavern of her mouth. Jessica gasped from the invasion as her knees wavered. She clung to Devlin's broad shoulders.

Devlin tore his hands from the wall and circled her waist. He crushed her against his length. Jessica gasped for air only to be pulled down by the erotic undertow.

Devlin's tantalizing fingers splayed against her ribs. Jessica inhaled deeply, her lungs expanding. His fingertips brushed against the underside of her breasts. Her nipples beaded with arousal, craving for Devlin's touch.

Alarm slowly trickled into her mind. What was she doing? Why was she allowing Devlin to touch her?

Allow? She was encouraging it. Jessica's hands balled into fists and she determinedly pushed away. Her chest rose and fell with each choppy gasp. She protectively folded her arms around her.

She felt the heat emanating from him in waves. She heard his ragged breathing and she could inhale a hint of his cologne.

'Look at me,' Devlin quietly commanded.

'I can't.' She didn't want him to know how his kiss had thrown her off balance. 'It's midnight.'

'Damn it...'

'I have to go. Goodnight.' She sidestepped him and walked toward the exit.

Devlin caught up with her immediately. 'Stop right now.'

Jessica was ready to give up – she couldn't continue this charade. It was tearing her up inside. Tears stung in her eyes and she blinked them back.

'Tracy?' Her mother's voice wafted into the corridor. 'We should leave. You have a busy day tomorrow.'

Jessica wanted to fall to her knees with relief. 'I'll be right there.' She tugged her arm free from Devlin's grasp. 'Goodnight, Devlin.'

'I'll take you home.'

'No. I'm not supposed to see you right now.' *Or kiss you, or be held by you...*

'Until tomorrow then.' He gently held her hand and raised it to his mouth. He brushed his lips against her knuckles. The simple gesture held a note of longing and promise.

Jessica wordlessly left and waited for her mother at the restaurant's exit.

'Are you all right?' her mother asked as they walked out into the cool summer night.

'I'm fine,' Jessica responded tiredly.

'I'm very sorry you had to go through with this masquerade. I truly am.' Her mother was silent until they reached the car. 'Do you think Devlin suspected anything?'

'I don't know. A couple of times I felt like I messed up, but he didn't call me on it.'

'Devlin isn't the kind of man who would.'

'That doesn't make me feel any better.'

'His suspicions don't matter anymore. The night is over and our mission is accomplished. Let's swing by your sister's apartment. She should be home by now. And you don't have to worry about any of this. Tomorrow, Devlin will marry Tracy and no one will ever find out what really happened.'

Devlin will marry Tracy...Devlin will marry Tracy. The phrase kept repeating in her exhausted mind.

She shifted in her seat and tried to get rid of the dull ache suffusing her body. She probably was getting the flu her mother had claimed she had. It would be a justified punishment!

After all, today she had deceived her family and friends, and she had tricked Devlin into unknowingly cheating his fiancée, and she had helped guarantee a wedding that was taking place for all the wrong reasons.

But that wasn't the real reason why she was tense and upset. If she were honest with herself, she would admit a darker secret. A darker sin. She was attracted to Devlin Hunter! She was attracted to her sister's groom. Jessica was sick with self-disgust.

She knew better. She knew Devlin was already taken and yet she allowed herself to get pulled in by his dynamic personality. She had accepted his kisses, not to help her impersonation, but because she craved his touch.

Her skin flushed with shame. Jessica leaned her warm forehead against the cold glass window. How could she have acted like that? Did she get into Tracy's character too much? Or did she indulge in an adventure because she wanted to be reckless for just a moment and not let anyone know.

Jessica wrapped her arms tightly against her abdomen, warding off the truth. She had done what she did because it was her only opportunity. Lurking under the guise of Devlin's fiancée offered the protection she needed.

What was it about Devlin Hunter? She disliked his type. Domineering, powerful and blatantly masculine. The men she dated in college were far from intimidating. She was drawn to their comfortable companionship. So why was she drawn to Devlin? Because he was forbidden?

Well, it didn't matter anymore, as her mother said. The wedding was in twelve hours and then Devlin and Tracy would be off on their honeymoon to Hawaii.

Jessica ignored the painful twist in her stomach. She had no right to be jealous – Devlin was bound to Tracy. He was never hers. She didn't want ownership of him.

If only she could play it smart. She would look for a job outside the Seattle area. She wasn't going to hover around the newlyweds, coveting her sister's husband. The marriage was going to have enough problems as it was.

'I'm proud of you, Jessica,' her mother said as she concentrated on the road. 'I know it was hard for you, but you really helped your sister.'

Jessica felt a glow shimmering inside her from the simple words. Her mom was proud of her and recognized that she could help out. Maybe the masquerade was worth all the hassle.

The car phone rang, blistering the peaceful silence. Jessica automatically picked it up. 'Hello?'

'Jessie?'

'Hey, Tracy. We were just about to swing by your apartment.'

'I'm not there.' Her voice held an odd note. Static and background noise blurred the phone connection.

Jessica frowned with concern. 'Where are you?'

'I'm still in New York. We've got a problem.'

'What kind of problem?' The muscles in Jessica's shoulders spasmed with tension.

'Nothing to worry about, but I might need your help.'

'Sure,' Jessica agreed, although not very eagerly. 'What do you need?'

'Can you extend the impersonation for just a little while longer?' she pleaded.

What was she saying?

'How much longer?' Jessica asked with growing suspicion.

'There's a good chance I won't make it to my own wedding. You're going to have to take my place!'

chapter four

Jessica's knees knocked together as the cathedral's double doors swung open, exposing her to the waiting mass of expectant guests. The swell of the organ blistered her ears and blasted through her fractured thoughts.

Jessica stood unmoving at the threshold. Barry tightly held her clammy hand in the crook of his arm. Her other hand shook as it clenched the pale orchids. The shaking matched the frantic rhythm of her chattering teeth.

'Tracy,' Barry hissed through his smile. 'If you take a runner now, I will destroy you.'

The threat galvanized her into action. She believed him, but it didn't calm her pounding heart. Jessica took a hesitant step forward, the toe of her shoe butting against the voluminous skirt of her beaded gown. She kicked harder, stumbling over the threshold.

At least the skirt hid the tremors attacking her legs, Jessica decided, wondering why she even cared. She must be on the edge of slipping into hysteria. Considering the circumstances, she wasn't surprised.

Her gown impeded her procession down the aisle. She paused as her shoe caught the hem of her skirt. Barry read the hesitation as indecision and he yanked at her arm. Jessica didn't acknowledge the sharp pain shooting through her shoulder. She didn't even glance at him. She couldn't see anything. Panic had fogged her senses.

Her ears buzzed as she stared straight ahead. She assumed the large, white spot was the clergyman. The man in black was Devlin. Her sight shifted and focused on him.

His black tuxedo did more than emphasise his lethal combination of elegance and masculine grace. He wore his clothes like armour containing, yet accentuating, his brute strength.

Devlin turned and she saw his ruthless expression. His dark eyes flashed dangerously. He managed to vanquish her brittle courage without the sweep of a sword, but with one slicing glance.

The harsh lines of his bronzed face tightened. His expression was aloof. Merciless. He didn't look anything like a groom. More like an executioner!

Jessica felt like she was walking to her doom. The heavy veil was as effective as any blindfold. The beaded gown weighed her down like chains. Barry hovered at her side like a guard in case she made an escape.

The walk down the aisle was agonizingly slow. And, strangely, it went by too fast. For one irrational moment, Jessica hoped Tracy would crash the wedding and would figure out some clever diversion so that they could switch back their identities.

That wasn't going to happen. She knew it the moment Barry knocked on the dressing room door at the church and declared it time. Jessica could have wept.

'It's not like you're marrying the guy,' Tracy assured her on the phone the night before. 'There's just a possibility that you might have to go through the motions at the wedding. We'll switch at the reception.'

Jessica wanted to scream out her refusal. But this was Tracy. The one who took care of her, the one who never asked for anything in return. 'I'm not sure about this. What if your plane is delayed again?'

'The airline said that the computer glitch is fixed. It's just a matter of time.' Tracy's voice was confident and Jessica believed her. She wanted to believe her. 'There's no way I can be delayed eighteen more hours.'

'Was the trip successful?' If it had been a waste of time, Jessica knew she would bawl at the injustice. She didn't understand why this trip was so vital to Tracy but, then again, she didn't understand business.

'I'm not sure yet,' Tracy hedged.

'The programmer is still dangling you?'

'Prog…? Oh, uh, yes. You know what those geniuses are like. *Prima donnas*, the lot of them,' Tracy rambled. 'But this trip will be worth the inconvenience.'

Jessica scowled. 'I don't know who the programmer is, but I hate him already. He's going to wreck your wedding.' She wasn't sure if this was a crisis in her twin's opinion.

Jessica gnawed on her lip as she voiced her deepest fear. It had niggled her troubled mind all day. 'What if Devlin figures it out?'

'He won't. He hasn't figured it out yet.' Tracy paused. 'Has he?'

'I don't think so.' Jessica didn't think this was the time to mention the possibility of her mistakes. She needed Tracy to concentrate on getting home.

'Then he won't,' Tracy blithely assured her sister. 'Don't worry about it.'

'I'm sure this is illegal,' she whispered into the phone.

'We have to go with it,' Tracy replied firmly. 'If they find out that I'm in New York, it will just be a matter of time before our deception is figured out. We can't back out now.'

'But if we go through it and then get caught…'

'I will be there,' Tracy said with absolute certainty. 'On time. I promise.'

Jessica blinked back to the present the moment Devlin's hand enveloped hers. She looked up to him, her eyes wide and terrified.

Devlin's grim expression rammed an icy fist to her throbbing heart. She watched as his dark, glaring eyes slashed down her trembling form. She felt like she was suffocating. The overwhelming scent of the flowers clogged her breathing passages. Dark spots popped in front of her eyes.

I'm going to faint. Oh, now there's a diversion. She wouldn't mind slipping into nothingness.

'Breathe,' Devlin muttered. He guided her hand to his firm mouth. The congregation murmured softly as they saw the groom brush his lips against the bride's wrist. No one noticed the threatening nip of his teeth to her cold skin.

The hour-long ceremony dragged for Jessica. She tried to concentrate, but her scrambled mind didn't allow it. She performed automatically and then wondered if she did it correctly, if she had said the right thing at the right time.

There were moments when Jessica would surface from the sluggish feeling, wondering how much longer she had to endure it. Were they in the middle? The end? Still at the beginning? Did she have to recite the vows or did they just do it?

It was all jumbled and she felt anxiety pressing onto her chest. Her breathing became rapid. She felt Devlin's strong fingers on her hand. She glanced at him and their eyes connected. She held onto his gaze, anchoring herself, focusing on the brown, enigmatic eyes.

'You may now kiss the bride.'

All too soon, Devlin flipped the veil. He held her pale face between his hands and kissed her. The brief kiss was hard with just a cruel twist, leaving her staggered.

What was going on? He gave the appearance of tenderness yet he punished her with his touch. Why?

'I present to you,' Father Woods' voice rang out, 'Mr and Mrs Devlin Hunter.'

Mrs Devlin Hunter. Jessica flinched. She felt like a judge had pronounced her death sentence.

Devlin escorted her down the aisle as the organ music invaded the cathedral with a cheerful recessional hymn. Jessica hurried to keep up with him, catching a glimpse of her mother's strained smile.

Her mother. Jessica's heart plummeted to her stomach. She was learning more about her family in these past two days than she ever had in her twenty-two years.

A part of her wished her mother had never had the heart-to-heart discussion in the cathedral's dressing room. Wished that she could see her mother through child-like eyes. But Jessica knew it all had to be said and that the conversation was past due.

Jessica had been on the verge of hyperventilating before the wedding as she waited for Tracy to make a dramatic entrance. As the clock ticked on, Jessica's courage failed.

She stared at her reflection in the dressing table mirror. She looked pale and fragile wearing the heavy wedding finery. 'I can't do this.' She could barely form the words with her bloodless lips.

'Yes, you can,' her mother patted Jessica's shoulder ineffectually. 'You must.'

'Just postpone it.' Jessica bowed her head. Shame filled her. Shame for failing, for being a coward. But the shame was stronger than her sense of duty. Knowing that, the shame grew stronger. 'Say that Tracy has the flu.'

'Jessica Ann, you will walk down that aisle.' The steely tone in her mother's voice caused Jessica to glance up. 'You're being extremely selfish.'

'Selfish?' she repeated in a high, astonished voice. She did everything Tracy asked. She went toe-to-toe with Devlin Hunter to help her sister. Just because she discovered she didn't have enough courage didn't make her selfish!

'Tracy is the one sacrificing her freedom marrying Devlin. She's doing it to protect her role in the company. The stronger the role there, the stronger she is in our family. She's doing all this to protect us. You, Tracy and me. Is it too much to ask for you to give up a couple of hours of your Saturday?'

Jessica's mouth hung open. She felt the attack was unwarranted. 'Tracy volunteered to marry Devlin,' she pointed out. 'She wanted to be in the business and if she doesn't want to be a part of the family, she has the option to leave. Tracy is sacrificing nothing.'

'I know about arranged marriages in the name of business. It is all about sacrifices – on the woman's part.' Lorraine Parks sat down on the embroidered stool next to the table. She leaned forward, demanding Jessica's attention. 'Do you think I wanted to get married? To Barry?' She sneered at the thought.

'In a way, yes,' Jessica shrugged. 'He gave us a better life than what we had after Dad died.'

Her mother scoffed. 'Better? We just moved into a high-priced neighbourhood. A gilt-edged prison.'

Jessica always felt that way. She was surprised her mother had the same experience. 'Why didn't you get out of it? It's not a real jail. Why don't you do it now?'

The older woman closed her eyes. The wrinkles and stress lines appeared in her perfectly groomed face. 'Because then I would have to go into a real one.'

Jessica frowned. Her mother in jail? Never! 'What are you talking about?'

'I'm talking about the real reason I married Barry.'

'I figured it was business.' Jessica was certain she didn't want any more information about the marriage between her mother and stepfather.

'In a roundabout way. As you know, for a short time I

worked for Barry as his social secretary. It was the only job I could do and the pay wasn't that great.' She shook her head from the memory.

'Times were tough,' she continued. 'I couldn't afford housing and food and utilities every month. I needed to find money somehow. Somewhere.' She looked past Jessica, past the room and into a place only she could visit. 'I never thought Barry would miss it. It was pittance to him,' she bit out. 'From the damn petty cash box. His petty cash could have paid our rent.'

'Mom?' Jessica's brain tried to put the scattered information together. 'Are you saying you...embezzled?' The idea was laughable. Her mother was a lady, not a criminal.

Lorraine Parks clicked her tongue against the roof of her mother. '"Embezzled" is such an ugly word. I borrowed the money and I had every intention of paying it back.'

Jessica bolted up straight in her chair. She admitted it! Her mother had stolen money. Her mother was a...thief. And she didn't show any remorse, any guilt. Jessica didn't know what to say. 'But he caught you?' she ventured.

Her mother gave a choppy nod. 'And he gave me an ultimatum. I had the choice of prison or marriage.'

'Why did he want marriage?' It didn't make sense. Barry Parks didn't need a wife. He didn't need anyone.

'He couldn't break through the social club set, no matter how hard he tried.' Lorraine's voice gained a snobby edge. 'I was his ticket.'

'You could have bargained your way...'

'Barry doesn't bargain,' she interrupted flatly. 'He didn't give me much of a choice. I knew marriage had the most advantages. I would be with you girls and be able to afford to give you the best.'

Jessica said nothing as she struggled with the drowning

guilt. Her mother had made the sacrifice for her. Jessica wasn't sure if the sacrifice was worth it. The disloyal thought increased her guilt.

'Now I wonder if prison would have been better,' Lorraine muttered. 'I think you girls suffered greatly under Barry's influence.'

Jessica stood up abruptly. She didn't want to think about her childhood in that soulless monstrosity of a house. 'We're grown-up now. Why do you stay?'

Her mother eyes were bleak. 'He still has the evidence of my mistake. He can destroy me.'

Barry's cryptic words zoomed into Jessica's memory. *I will blame your mother…because I can.* Her stepfather seemed to actually look forward to watching her mother squirm.

'If he finds out you're not Tracy,' she continued, her words bleeding with desperation, 'if this wedding doesn't happen, we're all going down.'

Jessica could well believe it. She knew Barry's ruthlessness. He had to have his way or destroy any blocks in the path to success.

Lorraine grasped Jessica's hands. The tight hold pinched and squeezed her fingers. 'You have to do this, Jessica,' her mother pleaded.

Jessica hesitated. There had to be another way. She frantically looked around the room seeking inspiration. *Think! Think!*

'You owe us.'

The three softly spoken words cut deeply. 'I know,' she whispered. And that was the bottom line. She owed them a tremendous amount and her mother was calling in all favours. If Jessica did not prostrate herself to her mother's wishes, Tracy and her mother would mark it down as a betrayal. It didn't matter if Jessica devised a foolproof plan and executed it brilliantly. She had to prove her love and duty by being thrown in the lion's den to save her family.

And what if Devlin discovers the charade and strips it into pieces? Would Tracy jump in and save her? Would her mother stand by her side or would she turn away?

What am I thinking? Jessica was horrified by her disloyal thought. *We will stick together. We're family. We're blood. It's just the panic talking. I'm just considering worse case scenario – and it couldn't possibly happen.*

Jessica gave a comforting squeeze to her mother's hand. 'I won't let you down.' She gave a trembling smile for good measure, pushing aside the niggling question of what her mother's response would be if she failed.

Guilt and duty were strong motivators, Jessica decided as her attention swirled back to the present. Nothing short of a fire would have sent her down to the altar.

'Tracy?' A voice far away slowly suffused her troubled thoughts. 'Tracy!'

Jessica's head shot up. Tracy was here? Relief flooded her tense muscles. At last! She frantically looked around but didn't see her sister anywhere. She whirled around, still searching, until her eyes clashed with Devlin's frowning face.

'What?' she barely breathed out. *Get me out of here. I can't take another second.*

'Tracy,' Devlin grated out. 'Are you ill?'

Jessica wanted to flop onto the floor and have a good cry. Tracy still hadn't shown up and she almost made another huge mistake. She bowed her head, hiding her tearing eyes from her groom. 'I'm perfectly well, thank you,' she replied. Her voice was hoarse and tight.

'That's highly doubtful.'

'Tracy,' her mother interrupted. She stepped between Jessica and Devlin. 'The photographer wants to take the pictures now,' she explained with an overly bright smile.

'All right, Mother.' Jessica allowed the older woman to drag her to the altar. She wanted to run in the other direction. Run from Devlin. No one would help her if she wanted to escape. Jessica rubbed her aching temple. Would the day never end?

The photo session was pure torture for Jessica. She knew her smile was strained as she performed pose after pose. She mindlessly followed every instruction the photographer suggested. *Stand here. Turn right. Tilt your head. Smile.* The photographer's commands were eerily similar to her mother and sister's. *Say this. Do that. Act like a witch. Pretend.*

'We need a picture of the couple signing the register,' the photographer announced.

Jessica broke out into a sweat. She could feel it trickling in the collar of her gown. *Wonderful.* She was about to commit fraud, in a church, and have pictures document every step. The day couldn't get much worse.

Jessica slowly made her way to the back room where Father Woods had the register laid out upon an old wooden table. She watched as Devlin signed it with aggressive strokes of his black pen.

He turned to Jessica and held out the pen. Jessica looked at it as if it were a poisonous snake. Her mother coughed delicately, jarring Jessica to reluctantly accept the pen. She fiercely concentrated on signing her sister's name.

'Right. That was the last one,' the photographer said, as he snapped an extra picture. 'We'll see you at the reception.'

Jessica gave an exhausted sigh. She was one step closer to freedom. She couldn't wait to escape from this ordeal, from this dress. From Devlin!

Devlin studied his nervous quarry with glittering eyes during the quick limousine ride to the elegant hotel. Why did he allow the wedding to happen? Devlin was used to following his gut instinct. It had served him well over the past few years. But that was when he was making deals and this didn't feel anything like business.

When he saw Jessica walk down the aisle, his gut instinct nearly knocked him flat. She looked exquisitely beautiful in the Victorian-style, ivory wedding gown. Her hair was scraped back away from her pale face. But it was the fine tremors wracking her body and the fearful look in her eyes that pulled his heartstrings. He knew he wouldn't stop the wedding. He couldn't turn her away from the altar. He felt the overwhelming need to protect her, to rip her away from Barry's grasp.

He was a fool. She looked helpless, vulnerable. Innocent. Her pure image was exotic to him and he couldn't stop wanting to believe it true. He should have refused her at the altar, in front of her family and community. It would definitely make his life easier if he didn't have a dependent wife in tow. He would also be one step closer to his goal.

Devlin still had time. There was the reception. He had every opportunity to toss her back to Barry before they cut the wedding cake.

He continued watching his pseudo-wife as she shifted uncomfortably under his gaze. What surprised him more than his actions was Jessica's determination. He couldn't believe Jessica had followed through on the insane charade. He still had the faint impression that she would refuse to pretend based on her naïve view of the world, on her strong belief of right and wrong.

He wanted her to be as innocent as she appeared, like a boy who wanted to believe in mythical legends. Obviously, she wasn't. She must want a piece of Parks Software Systems very badly. How much did her sister promise? What did Lorraine offer to sweeten the deal?

He shelved his brooding thoughts as the vehicle parked in front of the hotel. He stepped out and assisted his bride as she eagerly stumbled out of the limousine. Devlin hid his amusement as he grabbed her by the waist and prevented her from falling. She murmured her thanks while her wildly lit eyes focused on the hotel. She still thought the reception would be her salvation. Devlin shook his head. She was going to be terribly disappointed.

They entered the reception room to thunderous applause. Devlin watched as Jessica smiled brilliantly to no one in particular. She didn't demur as he escorted her the centre of the dais. Devlin knew she was vaguely aware of the reception ceremony. Her mind was filled with possible escape routes.

As the reception dinner progressed, Devlin was keenly aware of Jessica's nerves winding tighter and tighter. She pushed her fork around the plate through every course. She sipped continuously from her champagne flute. Jessica was always one beat off as she smiled and laughed over the well wishes and toasts.

'It is time for the bride and groom to dance,' announced the orchestra conductor.

Devlin wanted to laugh as he caught Jessica's cringe. He knew she had forgotten about the dancing. Well, he'd be nice for the moment and not try anything on the dance floor. She was upset and tipsy. He had the luxury of keeping his net trap slightly open. Victory was already his!

As he gathered Jessica into his arms, they circled around the dance floor to the sweeping rhythm of a waltz. He hated to admit it, but it felt good holding her. Her delicacy and subtle femininity tantalised him. He glanced down at her fragile features. His mouth twisted in a small, wry smile. She didn't even notice him as she continued glancing around the room.

The waltz faded to an end and the guests applauded. Devlin knew it was now time to dance with other members of the bridal party. As he offered his hand to Lorraine, Nicholas motioned for his attention. They exchanged a nod and a glance. He returned his attention to his mother-in-law, startling her with his triumphant smile.

Jessica gave up on small talk as she danced with the man who had caught her garter. Her mind felt so cluttered that she couldn't think of a coherent sentence. The man twirled her around, the heavy folds of her dress slapping her tired legs. As she turned, Jessica thought she caught a glimpse of Tracy. Her heart exploded with hope.

Please let it be her, Jessica prayed. She waited impatiently for the song to end before giving the man a polite smile and hurrying off the dance floor.

Where would she find her? Jessica marched to the door as she formulated her search plan. Possibly the ladies' room. She hurried to the area in the darkened hall. She swung open the door and found emptiness.

Jessica pressed her lips shut to prevent from calling out her sister's name. If one of the guests were here, they would wonder about her sanity. Jessica investigated every empty stall.

Where was she? It didn't make any sense. Did she imagine Tracy's appearance? Did she want her here so much she dreamed her up? Or was she finally losing her mind?

Jessica paced the bathroom linoleum floor. She would hide here, away from everyone. Away from Devlin. She could wait safely until Tracy arrived.

The door swung open. Jessica looked up expectantly, her heart choking in her throat. A gaggle of bridesmaids burst into the bathroom.

'Tracy! There you are. Devlin's looking for you.' They hurried her through the door. 'Time for you to go.'

No! Jessica tried to grab onto the doorframe but missed. She couldn't leave. She couldn't go into the suite – she'd never get out to make the switch.

Devlin appeared before her. Jessica shivered with fright. She had to escape – this was her last chance.

As if he could have read her mind, Devlin captured her hand. She watched silently as his large palm swallowed her cold, paralysed fingers.

She was trapped. Panic crashed around her. Jessica stared dumbly at their joined hands, unable to come up with a plan.

In a fog, the two said their goodbyes to the boisterous guests. Devlin led her to the lifts. He didn't let go of her even as the doors slid shut and the lift zipped up to the top floor.

The elevator halted. Her stomach heaved as she froze on the spot.

'Getting cold feet already, Tracy?' he mocked. 'A little late for that, don't you think? You already signed the register.'

It wasn't the paperwork she was worried about!

Devlin half-dragged, half-pushed her out of the lift. Her feet sank into the plush carpeting. She wished the rest of her body would.

Without warning, Devlin lifted her into his arms. Jessica squeaked out a protest and hung onto his shoulders. Her feet stuck straight out in the air as every muscle in her body stiffened.

Devlin chuckled. 'Just following tradition,' he said, cradling her closer to his chest. The heat billowed from his body and awakened her senses.

'Give me a little notice next time,' she mumbled, wishing he would put her down. Jessica did her best to ignore the husky sound of his laugh and the rustle of their clothes. She turned her head, warding off the intoxicating scent of his cologne. It was bad enough that she felt the hard planes of his shoulders under her hands.

She didn't want to notice. She couldn't handle her senses being on full alert. The only way she could cope was to shut down her senses and her mind. Fully realizing Devlin's sex appeal was not helping matters.

As they entered the honeymoon suite, Jessica cautiously glanced around. To her great relief, there was nothing crudely sexual. Or, for that matter, nauseatingly romantic.

The stylish décor whispered elegance and comfort.

The sheer curtains were pulled back, offering a night-time view of Seattle, but the darkness hid the picturesque view of the majestic mountains. The cosmopolitan lights didn't shine in to the room and offer relief from the shadows. Jessica shivered, wishing for the glaring, blinding sun.

Devlin slowly let her down to the floor, her small curves grazing every masculine angle. Jessica stood where he left her, not certain if she should hide in the bathroom or make a run for the door. Perhaps she could pretend she had forgotten something downstairs. That wouldn't raise his suspicions.

A mobile phone rang. She jumped, startled. The soft purr sounded like an alarm to Jessica's sensitive nerves.

Devlin smiled wryly. 'I'll just be a moment,' he promised, flipping out his sleek phone from his coat pocket. 'And then you can ravish me at your leisure.'

Jessica glared at him, deciding she wouldn't touch his last statement with a ten-foot pole. 'Who would be calling you on your wedding night?' She folded her arms across her chest, more as a hiding mechanism than an irritable gesture. 'For that matter, what groom would carry around his mobile phone?'

'Now you're sounding wife-like.' He turned away from her, ducking his head as he listened intently to the caller.

Her glare deepened until her eyes were narrow slits. She threw herself into action, her bumbling fingers detaching her train. She pulled off her veil, mindless of the hairpins tumbling to the floor.

'Thanks, Nicholas.' Devlin turned off the phone and discarded the piece of technology, tossing it onto the sofa. 'Here, let me help you with that.'

'No, no.' She dodged his hands. 'I've got it.'

'Are you going to deprive me of my husbandly duties?' His smile was downright wolfish as she tensed from the implication. 'Don't I deserve the right in assisting my bride out of her wedding gown?'

But I'm not your bride! She wanted to scream. Her breath hitched in her throat as he cornered her. She took an automatic step back. Her heel rammed into the door. She had no idea she was that close.

Devlin reached out and plucked the veil from her head. He tossed it to the side. Jessica's attention clung to the floating piece of netting until Devlin speared his fingers into her tight chignon.

Jessica stared at him, trying to find a way to make him stop without revealing her true identity. She had to make him stop. This wasn't right! No matter if she wanted one more kiss. One more touch.

She slicked her tongue across her parched lips. She gasped as Devlin bent down and chased her tongue with his own. Jessica darted her tongue back, bewildered when he followed.

He invaded her mouth, kissing her deeply. Tingling excitement flooded her bloodstream. Their tongues duelled and she opened her mouth wider. He filled her senses until they overflowed and her greedy mouth wanted more.

I shouldn't be doing this. The words slapped her mind, but her body wasn't listening. The coiling hunger deep in her tummy clamoured for attention. The sensation was unfamiliar but strong.

She placed her hands against his chest, determinedly ignoring the delicious warmth. Jessica had to put a stop to this and find an escape. Run back home where she could hide from Devlin's forbidding world and his touch that she found so addictive.

Devlin leaned into her, crushing her between the unyielding door and his hard body. He parted her legs with his knee. She fought the urge to rub against his thigh.

Jessica raised her hands to his head so she could push his head to the side. Her fingers skipped and threaded into his hair, abrading his scalp with her nails. Devlin shuddered, the motion rippling to her core. He devoured her with kisses, his wild mouth bruising her soft lips.

Devlin's blunt fingertips skimmed along the high neck of her gown, dipping over the lace edge. Jessica arched her throat as he curled his fingers around the fragile fabric and tugged. The rendering of silk and lace filled the pulsating air. She arched closer to Devlin, revelling in the freedom from the restricting style.

Jessica's lips clung to Devlin's mouth as he pulled away. Her jagged neckline was crumpled in his fists. She wordlessly swayed towards him. She didn't care about the wedding gown. Her skin craved his heat.

Devlin's eyes blurred with desire as he ripped the silky fabric with determined strokes. The atmosphere crackled. Jessica mewled with pleasure as the dress sagged and bunched to her waist. She imagined his bronzed skin pressed against hers, knowing the touch would be electric.

His eyes darkened as he noticed her pale breasts concealed in the wisp of ivory lace. He trailed the outline of her demi-cup bra with one long finger. His knuckles bumped against her nipple, which tightened in immediate response. He flicked open the clasp. The bra parted, exposing the rosy, aroused tips of her breasts.

Devlin groaned and roughly kissed her. Jessica returned his kisses, matching his ardour. He covered her breasts with his hands. She purred and stretched as he palmed them, rubbing the beaded nipples with the pad of his thumbs.

With a deep growl, as if he couldn't help himself, Devlin pulled his mouth away from her swollen lips. He brushed his mouth down the erratic pulse in her throat, and nipped lightly at her collarbone to her erotic delight. Devlin grazed the slope of her breast with the edge of his teeth before latching on to her ruffled nipple.

She thought she would melt under Devlin's expert tongue. Her entire being revolved around his magic touch. Liquid fire seeped into her, stoking the blue heat flickering to life deep inside.

Devlin turned to her other breast. She whimpered from the loss of contact. She arched and swayed, searching for something she couldn't understand. Somehow Devlin knew exactly what she craved, and pinched her swollen peak between his rough fingers.

The alternating touch heightened her arousal. Moist heat and hot friction. The seductive pull and the sharp pressure. She arched and bowed her spine, accepting the primal, yet complex, sensations.

Devlin trailed hot, wet kisses down her ribcage. She thrust her stomach out, eager for his mouth and wanting more. He dipped his tongue into her navel.

Jessica hissed from the audacious touch. Fire streamed through her as his warm, wet touch electrified an area deep in her stomach that had lay dormant. She clung to his shoulders as molten sensations stormed her body. Jessica looked down at Devlin. His dark head next to her hip made her quiver.

'How far are you prepared to go?' His voice vibrated on her against her navel. Her nipples tightened until they stung.

'Huh?' She frowned, unable to comprehend. 'What?'

Devlin rose from his crouched position. 'How far are you prepared to take this?' The victorious gleam in his eyes pierced her muddled mind. 'To pretend that you are Tracy?'

chapter five

'W-what are you saying?' Her heart pounded painfully against her ribs. Her mind screamed the obvious. He figured it out! But how? When? More importantly, what did he plan to do about it?

Devlin shook his head sharply. 'Drop the act, Jessica.' He wasn't going to put up with her display of ignorance.

She pressed her back into the door, trying to maintain some distance. The goal was impossible. 'I think you're confused.' She looked down, unable to maintain eye contact. She gathered her bodice and held it against her chest with her arm.

He trailed a finger along her throat. 'No, I'm seeing the situation clearly.' He circled her leaping pulse point with a taunting knuckle.

'I'm Tracy.' She took an exploratory step to the side. Her sweaty palm bumped against the doorknob. She grasped it as if her life depended on it.

'No, you're not.' He watched her through heavy-lidded eyes. His slumberous expression heightened her agitation. She was ready to explode.

'Perhaps you really are confused.' She quietly twisted the knob. It turned! 'You married me, the older twin.' She took another miniscule step to the side. 'Tracy Lynn Parks.'

His hands smacked the door, barring her escape with his sinewy arm. 'I know that was the name on the pre-nuptial agreement, the name on the Order of Service. The name on the register. Which leads me to wonder why it was the other twin walking down the aisle.' His face was millimetres away from hers. His hot breath blew the wisps of her hair and his glaring eyes commanded her to look at him. She unwillingly obeyed.

'How many times do I have to tell you that I am Tracy?' her voice squeaked out, as her hand spasmodically clenched the doorknob. Even though it was useless, she couldn't give up the possibility of escape. Devlin would have to pry her fingers off the cold metal.

'You can stop trying to tell me because it's not going to change the truth. I know you're Jessica.' His quiet voice was final. Nothing she could say would convince him otherwise. She still had to try.

'And I'm telling you I'm Tracy. You know what I think?' she improvised wildly. 'I-I think you're having second thoughts about this marriage. Yes, that's it! You're trying to blame your cold feet on something else.'

Devlin's eyes narrowed. 'I know you are Jessica,' he whispered coldly. 'And I can prove it.'

How could she possibly respond to that? She licked her parched lips. It took every drop of courage to reply, 'I'd like to see you try.'

Devlin rewarded her with a look that made her want to cower. What evidence did he have? It didn't really matter. She could already hear her jail cell swinging shut.

'The real Tracy is in a room on the floor below us.' He studied her face for any revealing nuance. 'Nicholas is with her now.'

She was right! She did see Tracy! Her sister didn't abandon her.

But Tracy was in just as much trouble as she was. It was up to Jessica to get them both out of this mess. What a role reversal! Was she up to it? It didn't matter – she had to do it. Jessica swallowed roughly, hoping that her mediocre acting skills would come through for this trial.

She laughed. A fake, humourless chuckle. 'You just kidnapped my bridesmaid? Thinking she was the bride? Oh, that's just great. Don't forget she's the one who has the flu. I hope Nicholas catches it.' Her eyes narrowed with feeling. 'It would be well-deserved punishment for dragging her into this.'

'You are Jessica.' Devlin moved imperceptibly closer. He pressed into her, reminding her of just how trapped she truly was. 'On our engagement, I gave Tracy a present. Pearl earrings from Australia.' His fingers flicked her bare earlobes. The touch scorched her. 'Pierced earrings.'

Damn! Her eyes widened as her simple mistake was exposed. He noticed her lack of earrings? What man noticed earrings? It was imperative to plant a seed of doubt. If she didn't do that, she could kiss her freedom goodbye. 'Just goes to show how unobservant you truly are. I've never had pierced ears. They're at the jeweller's right now, being modified to clip. I didn't tell you so I could spare your feelings. The earrings were a lovely gesture,' she tacked on the polite words, belittling the gift. Just as Tracy would have done.

Devlin's eyes gleamed. With admiration or with annoyance? 'What a cool liar you are, Jessica. You've learned well from your family. It's a shame you haven't a clue when someone is lying to you.'

Jessica frowned. Who lied? Was he just lying? Did he throw out the theory of switched sisters without having any basis for the accusation? 'What are you talking about?'

'You're very different from your sister,' he continued, studying her face. 'Tracy is cold and unfeeling. You, on the other hand, are passionate and respond wildly.'

He made it sound sexual. Is that what he meant? Jessica's eyes narrowed. 'Are you saying…?'

Devlin's smile was wickedly glorious. 'Tracy and I were never lovers.'

Jessica felt the blood drain from her face as rage mushroomed inside her. 'You – you monster!' she screamed, pushing at his chest, desperate to get away. It was like pushing a boulder. He easily grabbed her wrists and hauled her flushed against his length. His tuxedo rasped against her bare skin. His demonic laugh made her want to slap him.

'Monster? Is that the best you can come up with? Tracy would know a few names that would make a sailor blush.'

'How long did you know?' she whispered. On the ride to the rehearsal dinner? During the wedding reception?

She was close to tears, but she wouldn't give this man the satisfaction. She wouldn't show him how she felt. He would use it to his advantage.

'I've known from the very beginning.' There was no boastful pride in his voice. More like disappointment because she didn't turn out to be a worthy adversary.

'Oh, please.' She shook her head. 'Stop indulging in revisionist history.' If he knew the truth that early, he would have cancelled the wedding.

He shrugged, the move drawing her attention to his wide shoulders. 'It's true.' His bored tone clearly indicated that he didn't care if she believed him.

She looked up and glared at Devlin's stark features. 'Let me see if I can get this straight.' Sarcasm layered her voice. 'My relatives can't tell the difference between Tracy and me, but you can in one instant?'

'Maybe they're all blind and stupid.' His smile sent an alarm skipping down her spine. 'Maybe your relatives aren't sexually attracted to you.' He spared a glance at her bare breasts.

'You're not funny.' She tried to pull her wrists from his grasp. He tightened his hold. Her skin felt hot and raw from his touch. *All this to sign on a programmer. He couldn't possibly be worth this much trouble!*

'What did you say?' His menacing aura surrounded her like a noose. She was so scared she could hardly breathe.

Jessica gulped. Did she say that out loud? Impossible. She scanned his calculating eyes. There was no way she would reveal Tracy's plan. She would not ruin everything. 'I said let go of me.'

'No.' His intense stare unsettled her more than his domineering touch. What did he want? What did he see?

She coughed, wishing the nervous lump in her throat would disappear. 'This entire situation has gotten out of hand. Since you've had your bit of fun, let's just make the exchange of brides and you can go on your honeymoon.'

His sharp gaze didn't leave her face. 'Thanks,' he said slowly as he appeared to swiftly analyse the situation, 'but no thanks. I've decided I don't want the exchange.'

He had to accept Tracy! If he didn't accept the marriage, they would all suffer. 'Sure you do,' she wheedled. 'Tracy is just downstairs.' She frowned at another possibility. 'Or was that a lie?'

'No, Tracy is here.' His smile was less evil and more indulgent but it frightened Jessica even more. What was he up to?

'Then what is the problem?' She belatedly realized her voice had reached a high shriek, revealing her unravelling nerves. Much to her dismay, her hysterics made Devlin calmer and in command.

'This situation,' he indicated her wrists that he still held, 'suits me better.' Devlin showed no interest in letting go. He seemed quite content in suffocating her with his nearness.

'Better?' she squawked. He couldn't possibly mean that he wanted her! Wanted her as his wife!

He nodded. Devlin's face held a stony expression, yet his

eyes gleamed with an undefined emotion. 'I have to marry into the family. It doesn't matter which sister.'

It doesn't matter…Oh, the nerve of him! As if she was a product and not a human being! 'It matters to me,' she said through clenched teeth. 'Anyway, we aren't legally married,' she pointed out. She wouldn't marry him no matter what the incentive!

'That will be rectified immediately.' He pulled her away from the door and walked her to the bathroom. 'Start changing your clothes.' He let go of her wrists and gently pushed her until she stumbled on the cold tile floor.

'No.' She grappled at the sagging ragged ends of her gown and pressed them against her breasts. 'Why should I?'

'We're going to Las Vegas to elope.' He leaned against the doorjamb.

Jessica stared at him with astonishment, absently rubbing the raw spots where he had held her. He dropped the bombshell so casually. 'Like hell we are.'

'You will marry me.'

She held the gown tighter, as if it could offer her protection. 'You're the one who needs to get married,' she reminded him. 'I don't.'

'Actually, you do.' He stuffed his hands in to his trouser pockets as if he had all the time in the world to discuss the matter. 'It's in your best interest.'

Her brow furrowed with incredulity. 'Hardly.'

'I have proof that you signed a legal document while pretending to be someone else. We both know that is against the law and requires a jail sentence. And don't waste my time inventing ridiculous alibis. If need be, I will fly in a handwriting specialist.'

Dread attacked her senses. He wouldn't do that, would he? He must be bluffing. But he wasn't the kind of man to make false threats. He might be planning his retaliation off the top of his head, but Jessica noted he was doing a very thorough job. He must be an expert on revenge.

Devlin added his final touch. 'I will also implicate your family in the fraud. Just imagine what that will do to your social standing and to the family company.'

'There is no reason to do that!' she cried. 'You don't even know why we did it. It had nothing to do with you. We did our best to make the wedding run smoothly. If you look closer, you'll see that we did everything so you would get the CEO position.'

Devlin shook his head. 'Excuse me for not showing my gratitude. No one tries to pull one over on me. They live to regret it.'

'Believe me,' she venomously glared at him. 'I'm regretting it already.'

Her opinion didn't wound him in the slightest. 'And if you know what's good for you, you will not fight me on this.'

She knew she couldn't fight back. He had her trapped. Still, she couldn't prevent from asking, 'or what?'

'Or I will drag you back into the reception.' He reached out and she scurried back, not realizing he was grabbing hold of the bathroom door. 'What a sight you would be. It will be the final touch as I let everyone know how you, Tracy, and your mother committed a crime.' Devlin softly closed the door, leaving her standing in the middle of the marble bathroom. She flinched as the hushed click of the door reverberated like a gunshot.

Devlin kept a close watch on Jessica as they flew to Las Vegas. The private plane was a luxurious necessity. It charmed potential clients and intimidated envious competitors. The gleaming mahogany woodwork concealed the high-tech equipment he could never get away from. The taupe suede furniture complemented the soft track lighting and pale brown walls. 'Champagne colour' his last mistress called it. The supposedly world-weary mistress had gawked like a girl at her first carnival as she explored every corner.

Jessica didn't seem aware of the plane's optimum comfort. She showed supreme indifference to the extravagant surroundings. If it weren't for the periodic smile to the chic flight attendant, Devlin would have diagnosed that his bride was suffering from shock.

His bride. The term gave him more satisfaction than he wanted. He shouldn't think of her in that way. She was his concern for the moment.

What was it she said? He played the words in his mind. *All this to sign on a programmer.*

The moment she had muttered those words, he knew she was in trouble. Not from him, but from her own family. They had lied to her about Tracy's mission. They had made her an innocent accomplice and placed her in jeopardy.

Devlin gripped the glass in his hand. He stared down at it and swirled the amber liquid. He had acted on instinct, deciding he had to get Jessica out of Seattle and out of her family's proximity. Once Tracy and Lorraine's plans were revealed, once his true plans were put into action, everything would explode around Jessica. At the end, the blame would settle on her delicate shoulders.

But first he needed to understand why she had agreed to the masquerade. She wasn't the type to do it on a lark or dare. Was it just a favour she had fulfilled, or was she getting something in return?

She must be receiving some reward. After all, Jessica didn't blink an eye when he produced a hastily composed pre-nuptial agreement from his harried attorney. She had briefly glanced at the document and signed her name without saying a word.

Yes, Devlin decided. Her sister or mother must have promised something great to make her turn away the opportunity of his millions. He was curious to find out about Jessica's bonus.

'Jessica, you look like a lamb on her way to the slaughterhouse,' Devlin mused. Damn, why did he think of her in those terms? Lamb. Dove. Innocent. He was losing his edge.

Jessica tensed but refused to acknowledge that he spoke. Instead, she tucked her jeans-clad legs further from him, as though if she curled up in a ball she would miraculously disappear.

'You know,' he said conversationally, as he sipped the last dregs of his drink. 'I understand why Tracy made the switch. She had the chance to improve her career. I understand your mother's motives. She needed to make sure the wedding went through because she knows Barry would blame her.'

He watched as her jaw shifted. She chewed the inside of her mouth. To prevent speaking on her mother's behalf? Or to tame the anxiety shrieking inside her?

'But what were you to gain?' Devlin asked. What made her tick? What did she value above all else? He realized his interest was not just to analyse the situation. He shoved the troubling thought aside.

The silence stretched. He knew the quiet twanged on her nerves. 'It doesn't matter,' she finally growled out, refusing to look at him.

'Money? Stocks? I know, a cushy job at Parks. No entry level for you.'

She folded her arms across her chest and tilted her body deeper into the sofa. Jessica's nose wrinkled with distaste. 'Don't try to measure me by your own low standards.'

He smiled as the insult glided off of him. 'Then it must be something personal.'

She turned her head to face him. Her eyes flashed angrily. 'I hate to break it to you, but the reason is crystal clear. I was the only one who could make the switch.'

Devlin nodded in agreement. 'And you would help your sister just because she asked? Just like that?' He snapped his fingers.

'Yes, of course.' She frowned at him, wondering why he couldn't comprehend the simplest, most natural reason.

'What amazing loyalty,' he mocked. 'All in the name of sisterly love. I'm impressed. Do you often help your sister this way?'

Jessica seemed deaf to his derision. She looked out at the night sky. 'First time,' she sighed. 'And I botched it up badly.'

'Do you owe her something?' he persisted. 'Would she forgive some debt? Or was she blackmailing you?' Devlin's mouth twitched at the thought. Jessica was too young, too ingenuous, to have a shameful past.

'I owe her everything,' Jessica responded. Misery clouded her eyes. 'And it will take a lifetime to repay.'

'Aha.' He understood. 'The guilt factor.'

Her jaw muscle flexed. 'You know nothing about family obligations.' She spoke through gritted teeth.

Devlin ignored the acid eating in his stomach. 'I know it all too well. I can't imagine Tracy helping anyone unless it was business-related. And unless it helped herself in the process.'

Jessica visibly bristled. 'That is not true! You don't know her at all. Tracy took care of me when we lived in Barry's house. She didn't get anything from it, other than grief and trouble.'

'Took care of you how?' He propped his chin on his fist.

Her mouth snapped closed and she shrugged uncomfortably. 'She diverted Barry's anger,' Jessica mumbled, obviously not wishing to revisit the past. 'Played his mind games so I would be left alone.'

Devlin huffed with disbelief. 'You think you owe her for that?'

'Of course.'

'Jessica, Jessica,' Devlin shook his head. 'You are judging people with your own high standards. Tracy thrives on that kind of atmosphere. She feeds off mind games, enjoys finding out that she's better than the others. She wasn't doing you any favours.'

Jessica shot him a look of pure hatred. She grabbed the headset resting at the table nearby and jammed it onto her head, effectively covering her ears. 'That's your interpretation, Devlin,' she said, twisting the volume knob to the entertainment set. 'But then,' Jessica added in a raised voice to meet the level of music, 'you weren't there.'

Jessica was exhausted as they walked through Las Vegas airport. She felt as wrung out as a limp dishrag. It was the middle of the night and her nerves had passed the point of overdrive. As she passed a few slot machines, she wondered what her chances were of escaping. Maybe it was time to make her own luck.

As they stepped outside into the surprisingly cool Nevada night, Jessica looked around the car park. There weren't too many people around, who would make her disappearance more difficult, but it was now or never. Taking a deep breath, inhaling the dusty air, Jessica made a mad dash in the opposite direction.

She managed just a few steps before Devlin caught her. He grasped her arm with insulting ease. 'This way,' he murmured, assisting her into a black limousine. She wondered about his tone. There was no anger or impatience – more like kindness. No, she had to be wrong. Kindness and Devlin Hunter were two ideas that did not mix.

She didn't want to think about it. She had more important problems. She had to get away. The need to run away flowed through her blood. She didn't question it or the consequences. She just knew it had to be done.

As Jessica slid across the plush leather backseat, she lunged for the other passenger door. She yanked at the handle and discovered it locked. Devlin sat down beside her and closed the door, giving no attempt to prevent her escape. 'They are child-proof locks,' he said, flicking a button to raise the dividing window between passenger and chauffeur.

'I want out.' She gave a mighty pull on the handle before kicking the door with frustration. The limousine smoothly moved into the congested traffic.

'Don't be stupid, Jessica.' Devlin spoke to her as if she was a toddler and it did not improve her mood.

Jessica huddled into her corner and remained silent. Frustrated anger radiated from her tense body. The interior of the limousine crackled with a charged silence.

She stared out the window. Focused on anything but the calm and confident man beside her. She saw the many lights of the Las Vegas strip. Pulsating and flashing lights of every imaginable colour. Everything appeared to be either neon or glitter. It jarred her frazzled nerves.

'Running away won't change anything,' Devlin finally said, startling Jessica. He cupped her knee with his large hand. 'You impersonated your sister and signed a legal document.'

She tried to yank away from his hold but, once again, Devlin predicted her move. 'Then bring in the authorities,' she dared him. A judge and jury were beginning to hold a certain appeal. She would rather deal with the government than Devlin's brand of the law.

'I don't see the need,' he drawled. His thumb lazily

rubbed the side of her knee, branding her through the denim.

'And I don't see the need to drag me to the altar when my sister is willing to marry you.' She tried to yank away again but he proved difficult to shake off.

Devlin's hand crept up her thigh. The touch smacked of ownership. 'But she won't make a suitable wife.'

'Yes, she will.' Jessica winced from the whining desperation leaking through her voice. 'She understands the business.'

'She wants to marry me. You have to marry me,' he pointed out. 'You'll be easier to tame.'

Jessica sneered with distaste. 'You are just as vicious as Barry.' Her words hit its mark as Devlin's face tightened with anger.

'You will not compare me with Barry Parks.' His fingertips pinched her thigh. Realizing the betraying gesture, Devlin removed his hand. 'I showed you mercy.'

'Ha!' Was he kidding? He didn't know the meaning of the word.

'I could have uncovered your masquerade at the altar,' he ticked off his alternatives with his long, lean fingers. 'Discredited you and your family in front of all those important guests. Tossed you back to your stepfather. But I didn't.'

Jessica couldn't believe Devlin would even consider those possibilities. Her stomach tightened with fear. What kind of man was she marrying? 'And this is how I show my thanks for your "mercy"? By marrying you against my will?'

'I don't want your thanks.' His shark-like smile made her stomach twist. 'Your surrender will be more than enough.'

Her hand itched to slap him. Rip the smile off his face. 'I hate you, Devlin Hunter.'

He patted her leg and chuckled. 'I know.'

'I, Jessica Ann Parks, take,' she sighed with reluctance, 'Devlin Caleb Hunter, to be my husband.' Jessica rattled off the remaining vows. The minister didn't seem to notice her lack of bridal joy.

She looked around the small wedding chapel. The word 'tacky' wouldn't begin to describe it. She knew it was going to be a gaudy wedding the moment they drove up to the chapel. Maybe it was the advertisements offering an Elvis wedding that tipped her off. Or perhaps it was blue neon lights casting an unreal glow on the otherwise quaint architecture.

The interior offered the same schizophrenic design of charm and kitsch. Rows of white plastic lawn chairs faced the altar. The background consisted of white trellises and fake flowers dyed in unnatural hues. When she walked down the spotted brown carpeting to a recording of 'Here Comes the Bride', the only coherent thought she could form was that she had at least dressed appropriately.

Her faded baggy jeans and crumpled pink T-shirt were not exactly what every little girl dreamt of wearing to their wedding. Jessica knew her loosely plaited hair was untidy and her face shiny. She was no beaming bride!

Devlin looked much better, she grudgingly admitted to herself. His charcoal casual trousers and dark-green polo shirt quietly advertised his power and status. His legs were slightly parted, his feet braced. Like a man who knew he had won the war, but was prepared to draw his sword for the unlikely attempt to renew the battle.

Jessica wondered why the clergyman didn't question this unusual couple before him. Well, it was Las Vegas. He probably saw even more unusual brides and grooms every hour.

The ceremony was over in just moments. Devlin leaned down to kiss her. She quickly offered her cheek instead. The last thing she wanted was to suffer through his gloating kiss.

Jessica was thankful Devlin declined the wedding cake offer in their package deal, but all too soon it was time to signed the register. She watched Devlin write his signature on the form with the same determined expression he had worn during their long wait at the city clerk's office to apply for the license. He silently offered the pen to her. As she gripped the pink-plumed pen, her sense of *déjà vu* increased. Jessica wrote her real name on the register, each ink mark thoroughly crushing her spirit.

As Devlin spoke to the minister, Jessica fought the impending claustrophobia. She had never had the sensation before. Her heart raced as she struggled to breathe. The small chapel started to close in on her. The need to escape could not be ignored. Jessica bolted down the aisle, away from the altar, away from Devlin, and out of the building.

She dashed down the street with no plan in mind. Where would she go? What should she do? She swerved through the crowd, brushing by men hawking catalogues and brochures offering scantily clad women. Jessica made a sharp turn at the corner. A huge casino grabbed her attention. She surged into the building, vaguely aware of the vaulted ceilings and strangely dressed waitresses.

The casino bustled with activity and was incredibly noisy. The ringing of bells and clinking of coins scraped at her nerves. The scent of fried food made her nauseous.

She weaved through the maze of slot machines. The overload of her senses confused her. Her instinct to flee crashed into exhaustion. Jessica flopped onto an empty stool next to a gaming machine that made an irritating swooping beep. She laid her aching head on the cold, silver metal, struggling not to collapse.

A hand softly covered her shoulder. She sighed, this time with defeat. She knew it was Devlin. Was she ever out of his sight? Is this what her marriage would be like?

'What do you want now, Devlin? I just married you. Isn't that enough?'

'I want you to stop running away,' he answered.

'You're asking for a lot,' she answered, straightening away from the slot machine. 'Prisoners have a habit of running away. It's an instinct.'

'You're not a prisoner.' Irritation roughed his voice.

'Are we going to live as husband and wife? Under one roof?' *In one bed?*

'Yes.' His tone brooked no refusal. The man did not negotiate. It was his way, no matter what. The only question would be her acceptance of surrender.

'Then I am a prisoner.' She pressed her lips together. A bleak, soul-destroying future yawned before her. She had fought so hard to ensure she wouldn't wind up in a situation like her mother's. How could Fate play such a cruel joke on her?

Devlin sighed heavily. 'You're suffering from lack of food and sleep.' He assisted her to her feet. Everything will look better tomorrow.'

'Doubtful.' She took stock of her situation. She had no money, no friends, no way out. She was beaten. For now.

chapter six

The hotel suite completed her sense of Alice falling through the rabbit hole. She dragged her tired feet across the thick pearl-white carpeting, taking note that the walls were curved. As she headed for the bathroom, Jessica saw there wasn't a straight edge to be found.

'If it's all right with you,' Jessica said, eyeing the ruby bedspread with trepidation, 'I want a bath and then to go to sleep.'

'Fine.' Devlin tossed the key card onto a side table. 'I'll order room service.'

She couldn't stomach the idea of having a civilized dinner with Devlin. 'I'm not hungry.' Even if he force-fed her, she would choke on the smallest morsel.

'You haven't eaten all day.' His voice shimmered with disapproval. 'Hoping to collapse into an unconscious heap?'

'Now there's a plan.' She slammed the bathroom door shut and sagged against it. Oblivion sounded wonderful right now. Realizing she was finally in a separate room from her new husband, Jessica locked the door and breathed a sigh of relief.

The bathroom looked like a treasure box. The fixtures, commode, and sunken circular bathtub didn't just gleam in gold – they shrieked! The walls were a velvety purple. She slowly turned around, observing the décor with horrified fascination.

Jessica spotted a gold-filigree phone next to the sink. She frowned, considering the placement odd until she realized she could now call without Devlin breathing down her neck.

She hurried over to the phone and hesitated. She made a grab for the phone and paused again.

Why was she hesitating? This was her key to freedom. She could call someone and get out of this rotten mess.

But whom would she call? Her sister was probably still cooped up in a hotel room in Seattle. Her mother would be home, but what good would calling her do? The marriage had already occurred. All her mother could do was tell Barry what had happened. Barry was the only one with enough power to push for an annulment. If he felt like it and that wasn't going to happen.

Jessica walked to the bathtub on autopilot. She turned the faucet knob and stared at the hot, steamy water gushing out. The sense of absolute conviction seeped into her mind and poured through her chest.

She was well and truly stuck.

Jessica knew she would have to wait in her self-made prison until Tracy liberated her. That may be a while, since her sister would be too busy fighting her own battle. Tracy may not be able to free her. Devlin was infinitely more powerful than her older twin. He wouldn't let Jessica out of this sham of a marriage until he was ready.

And, from the sounds of it, that may be a very long while.

Jessica inhaled shakily. It was up to her. She had to get out on her own. She had to be smart so her family and Parks Software Systems didn't get hurt. She had to pick exactly the right time to break free.

Oh, God. Jessica cradled her head in her hands. She wasn't up to this. She was in over her head, fighting people who were smarter and more dangerous than she.

Devlin had money, power, influence, and a network of allies at his beck and call.

She barely had power over her unsteady nerves. She couldn't influence her future, let alone someone else's. No network was around to back her up.

The truth hit her squarely in the chest. She had no one.

Her body trembled as the horror dawned on her. She was on her own. Jessica pressed her hands against her eyes and wept.

Devlin peered out of the hotel window. He wasn't one to indulge in second-guessing, it was a waste of time.

And yet, he wondered if he had gone about the impromptu change of plans the wrong way. Why did he pick Las Vegas? Why did he insist on marriage? Why did he even care what happened to Jessica?

There were other options, but Jessica needed to get out of Seattle. She had to have the protection of his name. Devlin's mouth quirked at the thought. It was a very old-fashioned, very archaic idea – the idea also held a lot of truth. People would reconsider ganging up on Jessica if she had the Hunter name.

Not all people, Devlin decided, scowling at the Vegas strip and pushing away from the window. There were a few who'd hated who she was and what she represented, the Hunter name be damned!

He glanced at his watch. His bride had been in the bath long enough. Was she planning on staying there all night? Devlin rolled his eyes at the high probability.

He wouldn't allow it. Walking into the bedroom, Devlin noted the stillness. No sounds of water or muttered curses about him. Had she spent the entire time sulking?

He tapped the bathroom door lightly with his knuckles. 'Jessica, dinner's ready.' He frowned at the answering silence.

Devlin knocked harder. 'Jessica?' What was going on? He knew she was in there. There was no way of escaping through a window.

'Jessica, answer me,' he ordered. Did she fall asleep? She was exhausted. Or was it more than tiredness? Did he push her too far?

Alarm gripped his chest and he went into action. Devlin slammed his shoulder into the door. The wood immediately gave way. He plunged into the brightly lit bathroom. Steam curled around him like smoke as his ears filled with the sound of splintering wood and Jessica's shrieks.

'What are you doing?' she yelled, her arms and legs splashing wildly as she tried to cover herself. She lost her balance and sank beneath the soapy water. Jessica broke the surface, spluttering and spitting like a wet kitten.

'Why didn't you answer?' he practically growled. He strode to the tub, grabbed her wet arms and hauled her out of the tub. Devlin wondered about the relief streaming through his veins. Anger soon followed. He wanted to shake her for making him worry.

'Get your hands off me!' She slapped and kicked at him. He barely flinched from the impact. 'What are you? Some kind of monster?'

Devlin sighed, pressing her closer. His clothing was wet from her dripping body. 'I'm not about to ravish you.'

'Could have fooled me.' She reached around him and grabbed the soft terry robe on the bathroom counter. 'Put me down! Now!'

Deciding she wasn't going to go crazy on him again, Devlin lowered her to the ground. She quickly pulled the robe around her, going to great lengths to hide her body from him. It was a waste of time. He had got more than an eyeful of her slick feminine curves.

Devlin scowled at her attempt to hide from him. 'There's no need to go into a virgin bride act.'

'It's not an act,' she answered stiffly, refusing to look at him. She fluffed her drenched hair with her fingers.

Devlin stared at her. This could not be happening. 'You're a virgin?' he asked, reluctant to find out the answer.

'Yeah.' She flashed him a look of pure dislike. Her face was bright red from the steam and embarrassment. 'I was saving myself for my wedding night. What a mistake that turned out to be!' She marched out of the room.

Devlin raked his hair with tense fingers. Great. He had just forced a virgin to marry him! He was beginning to feel more like the monster Jessica claimed him to be.

Worse, he was actually pleased that she was an innocent. He wanted to be her first. Her last. Her only.

Damn, why was he thinking like that? His fingers gripped his skull for a moment before he firmly stuffed his fists into his trouser pockets. Knowing he had to be calm and controlled, Devlin strolled out of the bathroom.

'Have you finished having your temper tantrum?' he asked nonchalantly.

Jessica stomped her bare foot. 'I am not having a temper tantrum. I think I've been a very good sport about this.'

He arched his eyebrow. 'You're kidding me, right?'

'No.' She glared at him. 'Considering that I would rather be strangling you right now.'

Devlin chuckled. 'I admire your restraint.'

Jessica's eyes narrowed into angry slits. 'I'm going to bed. Alone!'

'A wise decision.' Devlin nodded. 'Goodnight.'

She tilted her head and studied him. 'What are you up to?'

'Nothing,' he replied as innocently as possible. 'I have a few business calls to make.' After that, he would consider his next plan of action.

He saw Jessica's frown deepen. Devlin couldn't help this unfamiliar need to tease her. 'Would you like me to tuck you in?' He closed the door as she threw a pillow at him with all her might.

She lay tense in the bed. This wasn't what she dreamed her wedding night would be like. She had hoped for somewhere romantic and personal. With a husband she liked!

Tears stung her eyes and she blinked them away. She wouldn't show any weakness. She was not weak. Just at a loss. But not for long. She would rest for now. Then, when Devlin fell asleep, she would sneak out. Devlin had to sleep eventually, didn't he?

She stiffened at every sound within the hotel suite. She wasn't sure what she was expecting. She thought Devlin would barge in and claim her. He probably knew she would claw his eyes out if he tried. And Devlin was smart enough to know that if he tried to overwhelm her with a smooth seduction, she would yell at him until his ears rang.

But the ignoring? What was that all about? He had said just a couple hours before that he was sexually attracted to her? Was that a lie? Probably. So why did the knowledge hurt?

Why did she care? She should be relieved. With an indignant sniff, she shifted to her side and drifted into a troubled sleep.

The bubbling trouble eventually foamed until it dissipated altogether. She fell into a deeper slumber, feeling safe and secure. She sighed softly and snuggled into the warmth.

Her hand rested on smooth, firm skin. The touch was unfamiliar, but it didn't frighten her awake. The steady heartbeat lulled her senses.

A gentle finger scooped a wayward curl from her face. She pondered at the tenderness, unable to recall the last time someone had demonstrated affection to her. She blinked awake, her mind fogged from sleep.

The edge of his thumb grazed the moist skin under her wet eyelashes. Tears? She hadn't realized she'd cried in her sleep.

She glanced at Devlin. His face was next to hers. She couldn't decipher his mood. The bedroom was dark but a strange feeling suffused the atmosphere.

Devlin lowered his head and brushed his mouth against her lips. Her nerve-endings sparkled with life. Her heart expanded and she returned the kiss.

Devlin continued giving gentle, slow kisses from one corner of her mouth to the other. Her lips parted of their own accord. Devlin speared his tongue into her welcoming mouth.

She felt light and airy. Buoyant. She opened her mouth wider, wanting more of him, enjoying his taste.

Her senses awoke with a start as his clever fingers parted the lapels of her bathrobe. His fingertips outlined her breasts. Her skin tingled as her blood fizzed with delight.

But her sluggish conscience was perturbed. She knew she shouldn't do this. She wasn't sure exactly why. 'Devlin...' She shifted, concealing her nakedness.

'Ssh.' His head sloped down and he flicked her nipple with his tongue. Her fingers clenched in his hair. Her nipples tightened. Heat billowed in her abdomen.

These sensations were new to her. She felt hot but her body shivered. Her ultra-sensitised skin needed to graze against his hard flesh.

Her body's reaction frightened her. Her heart thudded in her ears. Her rough breath scratched her throat. Her mind dissolved into sludge as she responded instinctively to his touch.

'Uh...Devlin...' Jessica wasn't sure what she wanted to say. She felt like she was on the threshold of a life-altering moment. She wanted to cross, to make the important step, but fear of the unknown held her back.

Devlin's head rose and he peered into her wide eyes. He reached out and cupped her face with his large, gentle hands.

Jessica burrowed her cheek into his palm, knowing that Devlin would guide and protect her.

Her eyelashes fluttered down as Devlin leaned forward and brushed his lips against her eyebrow. He bestowed a kiss on each eyelid with the lightness of a butterfly's wing. Jessica's breath caught in her throat. She had never felt so cherished.

Her breathing resumed in a ragged gasp as Devlin's fingers trailed from her jaw line down her throat. He caressed her curves until she couldn't lie still. Devlin closed his lips upon her breasts and suckled with a steady pull. Jessica's nipples stung and burned.

'Oh…' Her hands unclenched his thick hair and fell onto his bare shoulders. Her fingers dug into his skin as he moved his attention to her other nipple.

Devlin continued his slow, sensuous journey. His mouth was firm and gentle as it discovered her secret delights. His hands coaxed and quietly demanded responses Jessica didn't know she was capable of giving.

When she began tossing her head from side-to-side, Devlin deftly tested the wetness between her thighs. Jessica moaned mindlessly from the touch. She followed the ancient feminine instinct and parted her legs wider.

Devlin nudged against her. Jessica's eyes widened. Now she understood. She wasn't afraid of the act of making love. She was afraid of this moment of surrender.

And she gave it to him unconditionally. He swiftly made his claim, carefully embedding into her feminine core. Jessica stared into his harsh face. His intense eyes silently demanded that she was his. There was no going back. Jessica couldn't deny it, but she couldn't voice it either. She glanced away, ducking her head into the crook of his shoulder.

He pushed against her maidenhead. Jessica gasped at the

sharp stab of pain from the invasion. She tilted her hips, trying to find comfort. Devlin tensed, shuddering like a racehorse at the gates.

'Jess!' It came out as a tortured groan. He surged forward and she met his thrust. Devlin increased the tempo, pounding and retreating fiercely, until Jessica thought she would lose her breath.

She felt a delicious dizziness. Energy formed and zoomed to the centre of her body. Pleasure-pain swirled and tightened until it burst into blinding light.

Jessica heard a keening cry that seemed far away, but yet it sounded just like her own. A hoarse shout followed. Devlin collapsed on top of her.

She blinked the room back into focus. Her heart throbbed in her ears. Her body shook from the aftermath. She pushed away the troubling thoughts storming her mind. Jessica knew she didn't have the strength to consider the reasons and consequences of her actions.

Instead, she snuggled deeper into her askew pillow and closed her eyes, shutting out everything. She couldn't shut out Devlin as his body heat warmed her bruised and awakened skin.

Jessica was too exhausted to complain or push him off. She didn't want to, secretly enjoying the intimate embrace. Jessica relaxed and allowed Devlin to surround her fully as she fell into a sated slumber.

Devlin snapped down the corner of his newspaper. 'I see you're experiencing the morning after,' he commented, as they sat across from each other on his plane.

Jessica scowled at her husband. Her toe tapped to a pagan beat. She fought the need to bridle at his innuendos. To rear back and give him a good, swift, well-deserved kick.

'I refuse to deal with your sulking again.' He folded his

paper and tossed it on a chair next to him. 'You might as well tell me what's bothering you.'

'I've been practically kidnapped,' she said with tight fury. 'Forced to marry someone I find detestable, and consummate this joke of a marriage. Why should anything bother me?' she ended sarcastically.

He watched her with a hooded expression. 'Is that all?'

His words unleashed more of her anger. 'Well, now that you mention it, there is something else. I only planned on getting married once. A beautiful, intimate wedding. Getting married to the man I love. Instead, I get a cheap Las Vegas wedding to *you*. And I'm wearing this…this…' she tugged at her wedding ring and threw it at him. It missed and hit the plane's wall with a thud.

He didn't watch the ring careening in the air. His gaze steadied on Jessica, his expression never altering. 'This?' he prompted.

'This monstrosity of a ring,' she hissed, losing all control of her anger. 'It's not even mine! It's my sister's leftovers.'

'Ah.' His eyebrows arched with supreme masculine understanding.

That's all he had to say? And the way he said it made her suspicious. 'What do you mean by that?'

'I see what's bothering you.' He nodded imperceptibly. 'It's to be expected.'

She sighed with frustration. 'I should hope so. I just spelled it out to you.'

Devlin gave a dismissive wave of his hand. 'That's all smoke and mirrors. You're still keyed up about last night.'

'No, I'm not.' She folded her arms across her chest. Trust a man to bring sex into an argument about feelings.

He dramatically clasped his hands to his chest. 'Yes, my darling,' he said in a mocking, dutiful tone. 'It was special. The earth moved. The angels wept.'

Conflicting emotions besieged her. 'Shut up.'

'Isn't that what you want to hear?'

In a way, it was. She wanted their union to be important, to have more meaning than a legal technicality he could now tick off his to-do list. 'No,' she answered, knowing she would never in a million years let him know how she felt. 'I want to hear that it won't ever happen again.'

'Be careful.' He shook a chiding finger at her. 'You might get your wish.'

'I was celibate my entire life until last night,' she replied sweetly. 'I'm sure I can handle it throughout our brief marriage.'

Devlin smirked. A knowing smirk that made her want to scream. Instead, she fumbled open her seat belt and rose from the leather couch.

'And since the event wasn't cataclysmic to you,' she said hoarsely, her throat clogging with emotion, 'I'm sure it won't be a hardship.'

Devlin instantly rose from his seat and blocked her way. 'Get away from me,' she muttered. She was close to tears again and needed to hide. Her pride was on the verge of shattering.

Her new husband was not one to take orders. He curled his arm around her waist and dragged her against his hard chest. She tried to push away but he captured her arms.

'I will only say this once,' he growled softly in her ear. 'You and I will share a bed every night.'

'I wouldn't want you to suffer.' Acid eroded every word she uttered, hating the way she shivered in his arms. Despising her weakness in the face of his strength.

'Last night…' He paused, the hesitation so un-Devlin Hunter. 'Last night may have been your first time, but it was also my first time with a virgin.'

She stopped herself from looking into his eyes. She

wanted to know why he had told her that. Why he felt the need to reveal that part of him? Devlin didn't reveal anything personal.

'All right,' she whispered. She jumped as he placed a soft kiss at the corner of her eye. The gentleness electrified her senses more than any passionate embrace.

'Now be a good little wife and ask the attendant for some coffee.' He patted the curve of her hip and released her. She hesitated at Devlin's change of moods.

'Good little wife?' Jessica walked toward the kitchen. 'You're pushing your luck.'

'You have no idea,' Devlin muttered as he sat down and opened his newspaper.

They landed at the Sea-Tac airport later that afternoon. Jessica sighed with relief as she and Devlin walked through the airport corridors. She searched for Tracy, who would be impatiently waiting for the plane.

She was now on her own turf, Jessica silently decided as she hurried around the travellers. Devlin walked besides her, slicing his way through the crowd effortlessly. She was home. Soon she would be back in familiar surroundings and she wouldn't feel so unequal.

Devlin and Jessica walked across the glass hallway that connected the airport to the garage. Jessica frowned and scanned the crowd milling around. Tracy was nowhere to be found.

She silently walked to Devlin's McLaren F1. Jessica would have preferred a taxi or a bus. Unfortunately, she had no money on her. She couldn't wait to regain the purse that held her credit cards. She looked forward to taking care of her own transport. She wouldn't have to rely on Devlin for anything.

She automatically walked to the correct side of the sleek

machine and allowed Devlin to swing open the car door. A thought suddenly occurred to her.

Jessica took a step back and studied it. 'It was the car.' She glared accusingly at the machine.

Devlin looked down at her, patiently waiting to assist her into her seat. 'What are talking about?'

'That's where I made my mistake.' She pointed at the offending hunk of metal. 'This stupid car.'

'First of all, this isn't a stupid car. It's a McLaren F1.' He had a give-me-patience look that one would find on an anointed teacher informing the ignorant.

'Is this where I'm supposed to genuflect?'

Devlin flashed a rare smile. His eyes gleamed with amusement. Jessica's chest blossomed with heat. 'And, secondly, I knew it was you the moment I saw you.'

Jessica spared him a disbelieving glance. 'What tipped you off?'

He studied her face intently. 'Your eyes,' he replied roughly, as if he was revealing too much. Too much about him. But that didn't make any sense.

She made a face, wanting to break the intensity wrapped around them in the cavernous garage. 'My eyes are the exact shade as Tracy's,' she lightly replied. 'Try again.'

'Your eyes are very different. They advertise your every thought, your every emotion. Your every desire.'

Jessica felt the scarlet blush start from her toes and zoom up to her forehead. The tips of her ears burned with embarrassment. 'They do not,' she muttered.

'Yes, they do.' He leaned closer, finding pleasure in the sexy teasing. 'Your eyes turn the bluest shade when I…'

'OK, that's enough.' She didn't think she could turn any redder. She particularly didn't want him to think she enjoyed his full attention.

'Are you sure?' The gleam in his brown eyes danced

knowingly. 'Didn't you want to hang around the airport a little more in the hope that your sister would come and rescue you?'

'That is not what I was trying to do,' she said stiffly and ducked into the car. 'Obviously, your eye-reading talents are not that great.' She gnawed on her inner lip over his apparent ability to read her like a book.

'Whatever you say, Jess,' he said with a smile and closed the door.

Jessica clicked her seat belt in place and wondered why Tracy hadn't appeared at the airport. Jessica was surprised and a little hurt. Wasn't her sister concerned? Perhaps Tracy was still 'detained' under Devlin's orders.

Jessica waited until they left the car park before asking, 'Did you ever let Tracy leave the hotel? Or is she meant to waste away because she pulled one over you.'

The corner of his eyes crinkled. 'Tracy was not held against her will. We kept her away from the reception, that's all.'

Then where was she now? Why hadn't she called the Las Vegas hotel?

Jessica was beginning to feel abandoned. Tracy knew where she was, knew that she needed help. Did her twin decide not to because Jessica had failed?

Jessica pushed the thought away. She didn't know where the disloyal idea came from. Probably from Devlin's snide comments. 'Where are we going?'

'Home.'

Home. The term had never quite defined Barry's house but, right now, she wasn't going to quibble about semantics. The mansion would offer some protection. 'You can drop me off at my bank and I'll take a taxi home,' she offered. Now was as good a time as any to distance herself from her husband. She didn't want him to get used to ordering her around.

'You're living with me,' he said with absolute certainty.

Was he insane? They were legally married. They didn't need to act like man and wife. 'That wasn't agreed on.'

'Yes, it was. It was a part of our pre-nuptial agreement. The one you signed on the plane before flying to Las Vegas.'

Jessica rested her head against the car window. She really wanted to bang her skull against the glass. She didn't recall that piece of information. But, then, she had only given a cursory glance to the document. Another idiotic move on her part.

But, at that moment, Devlin held all the control. She was afraid to disobey his commands. Afraid to find out the consequences. Not much had changed, although she didn't feel the absolute terror like before. How strange…

She wondered about that as the sports car ate up the miles. The glass and metal office buildings became smaller and architecturally monotonous. Ribbons and ribbons of evergreen trees swept by her before she noticed they had thickened into forests and hills.

The hills began to grow and the road started to wind around sharp inclines. *Uh-oh…* Jessica wasn't too sure about the location of her new home. It was beginning to look isolated.

'Where exactly do you live?' she finally ventured as they zipped by a few horse ranches and small farms complete with red barns. She didn't remember this part of the Seattle area.

'We'll be there in a few minutes.'

She looked up as a colourful hot air balloon drifted lazily in the cloudless sky. A dark craggy mountain loomed ahead. 'You live on a mountain?' Her heart sank. It made sense. There was something very hard, unmovable, and remote about Devlin Hunter.

Devlin grinned. 'Not quite. I live in the valley. I own a vineyard.'

'A...vineyard?' That was news to her. She considered him to be a man who preferred the surroundings of computers and numbers. She didn't think he would like to deal with nature and all her uncontrollable glory.

'A very small one. For the moment.'

Now that sounded like the Devlin she knew. Anything he touched would become something great and powerful. Too bad she couldn't say the same about herself!

'You know, I'm more of a city girl,' Jessica confessed as they drove by flat farmland. The irrigation system sprayed over the vegetation like giants fans. She wasn't sure what to expect, but she didn't cope well with creepy-crawly things and pollen.

'I think you'll appreciate my home. Our home,' he corrected. The two simple words made her breath easier. 'Here we are.' He drove his car up a steep hill and turned at an impressive wrought-iron gate. The iron was worn and rusty in some spots, but it didn't diminish the contemporary weaving vine design.

Devlin opened the gates with the click of a button, the movement scattering the hissing geese off the bumpy driveway and into the vineyard. Jessica didn't know much about winegrowing, but the small, stubby plants looked a lot like miniature leafy trees than grapevines. Old, grey wooden stakes dotted the field, stretching thin metal wires that controlled the vines.

She hazarded a guess. 'This is the vineyard?' She didn't know the first thing about wine. The number of glasses she had had in her lifetime could be counted on one hand.

'Like I said, it's very small. This vineyard produces only white wine. The other wineries in the area have vineyards on the other side of the Cascades mountains in Columbia

Valley.' He nodded to his left. 'Over there is our new oak-aging cellar.'

Jessica dutifully 'oohed' and 'ahhed', wondering what oak had to do with anything and why it was aging. The modern building was rather non-descript so she wasn't sure why Devlin had pointed it out. She hid her smile as Devlin proudly informed her about the last harvest bounty.

The McLaren F1 followed the meandering road, passing by fat trees with ropey trunks and gnarled roots bursting from the soil. 'How long have you had this place?' Jessica asked as they drove under a canopy of purple-leafed trees.

'It's a recent purchase,' Devlin informed her as they manoeuvred around a shallow pond, complete with a rickety, arched bridge. 'I bought it from a friend of mine who retired from the high-tech world and saw this vineyard as a hobby.' He turned to Jessica and grinned. 'He got discouraged very quickly.'

'What makes you think you won't do the same?' Jessica asked. She has always been a the-cup-is-half-empty kind of person.

'I never get discouraged.'

Jessica rolled her eyes at his blatant confidence. The main house immediately caught her attention. She stared at the breathtaking view in front of her. It was a contemporary structure of native stone, wood and glass. The architect had managed to convey hospitable warmth with the cold elements by using a fusion of Asian and Pacific Northwest designs.

She could already tell that the interior would be drenched in the rare summer sunshine. Giant windows faced the lush vineyard and the hills were dotted with evergreen trees. Jessica imagined one could easily see the first steps of a craggy, magnificent mountain from the opposite side of the house.

Her car door swung open. Jessica jumped, startled. She fumbled with her seat belt, unwilling to take her eyes off her new home.

'What do you think?' Devlin offered his hand and assisted her out of the low-slung machine. Jessica sensed a deeper meaning behind the casual words.

'It's…it's…' She wasn't sure how to describe it. The word 'beautiful' was too banal. 'It fits perfectly with the surroundings.'

'I'm not sure that's a compliment coming from a city girl.' Devlin smiled as he escorted her to the steps. He wrapped his arm around her waist, drawing her close.

For once, Jessica didn't feel the need to push him away. 'I think I can handle the country life if it means living here. But I don't know much about running a house.'

Devlin shrugged. 'Nothing to worry about. I have a live-in married couple who take care of the house. You'll like Rodgers and his wife.' He rang the doorbell. The low gong-like bellow resonated inside.

'Do I get a key?' she asked and instantly regretted the question as Devlin frowned. She didn't want to spoil the tenuous truce.

'Of course. You're not a prisoner. You're the woman of the house. My bride. Which reminds me.' He bent down and swept her into his arms.

'Devlin!' Her fingers hooked into his soft shirt. She curled her knees around his strong arms.

'Oh, that's right. I was supposed to warn you, wasn't I? I'll remember that the next time.'

'There won't be…' Her voice trailed off as she saw a familiar silver Cadillac whip into the driveway. Gravel sprayed everywhere.

Jessica's fingers gripped even tighter into Devlin's shirt. She instinctively leaned closer into his solid chest, noticing

Devlin's body humming with tension.

The Cadillac was not exactly the Cavalry coming to her rescue. The driver's door shot open. 'What on earth is going on here?' Barry's voice boomed, echoing in the silent outdoors.

Jessica wished she could hide and disappear. The front door opened and an older man, who she assumed was the butler, stared incredulously.

'Hi,' she said through a tight smile. 'I'm Jessica Parks – no, Hunter. I'm Devlin's bride and the man screaming at him is my stepfather.' OK, why did she feel the need to add that?

'Jessica?' the man asked and shook his head. 'You mean Tracy?'

Jessica felt her face turn crimson. She should have realized some questions would remain. 'Slight change of plans. Different bride, same last name.' She pasted on the stunning smile, certain it had a manic edge to it. 'And you are?'

'Rodgers. Your butler,' he reluctantly answered, probably wondering at the mental health of the new mistress of the house!

'Pleasure to meet you, Rodgers.' She wished she could offer her hand, but she was holding on to Devlin for dear life.

'Likewise,' Rodgers muttered. He silently tried to gain eye contact with Devlin, hoping to get a clue of what was going on.

Jessica brilliant smile slipped a notch. So much for a fresh start in her new home! She was going to strangle Devlin when she got the chance.

chapter seven

'Put me down,' Jessica hissed at Devlin through clenched teeth. She tried to scissor-kick but it just made her feel even more ridiculous.

'I'm just following tradition,' Devlin responded as he strode through the front hall, ignoring her blustering stepfather.

'Hunter!' Barry yelled. He followed them into the mansion uninvited.

Jessica craned her neck, trying to catch a glimpse of her stepfather. She discovered the entry hall had cathedral ceilings and a stunning modern glass chandelier. The focal point was the sweeping curve of stairs to the next floor. The ebony-coloured banister and vermilion carpeting mimicked the colour scheme of the stark floral arrangement. A museum-quality painting hung nearby, the abstract design making her think of Chinese calligraphy.

She caught the eye of the butler. The man quietly twisted his hands with indecision. 'I don't think we need anything right now.' She offered him an assuring smile.

Rodgers appeared dubious. He cast a glance at Devlin, but was unable to catch his attention. Devlin was too busy glaring at Barry.

'I'll let you know,' Jessica promised. The butler scurried away. She bet her savings he would be standing outside the door, his finger hovering over some emergency button. This household would soon learn that the Parks were like this every day!

'Sit down, Barry,' Devlin suggested as he carried Jessica

into a formal living area. The spacious room emphasized the thick wood rafters and an enormous stone fireplace. The floor-to-ceiling windows were bare of curtains and displayed the spectacular view of the vineyard.

The living room was an edgy union of sleek, restrained architecture and outrageous modern art. Jessica wondered how much the room reflected its owner. The Picasso-inspired throw pillows softened the extreme lines of the bronze sofa. A pair of brown Italian leather armchairs huddled near the frosted-glass-and-steel side-table. The plush terracotta ottoman gave a luxurious relief to the aggressive shape of the fireplace, while the black suede chaise offered refinement to the distressed wood floor.

'I would offer you something to drink,' Devlin said to his stepfather-in-law, 'but you are intruding on my honeymoon.' There was an underlying bite to his words, which Barry seemed to miss.

'Who the hell cares about honeymoons?' Barry's voice blistered the tranquil atmosphere. 'I want to know what game you're playing.'

Devlin lowered Jessica to the worn wooden floor, his eyes never leaving hers. 'No game.' He seemed reluctant to step back.

Jessica looked away. Her blood fizzed with excitement over the mere brush of his skin. She had to start controlling her reactions. If he realized how his touch affected her…

'Bull,' Barry said succinctly. 'You were supposed to marry Tracy. You marry Jessica without anyone knowing. Our plans are ruined!' The older man's face blistered with ruddy colour.

'Not necessarily.'

'Don't you get it? Pay attention to me, damn it!' Barry snarled. "The wedding isn't legal.'

Devlin turned around and faced the older man. 'Jessica

and I flew down to Las Vegas and made it legal. I am married to a Parks. I have fulfilled the terms of the contract.'

Barry's eyes brightened, like it always did when a plan succeeded. 'Good, good.' He rubbed his hands and flashed a look at his silent stepdaughter. 'Why the switch?'

Devlin paused. Jessica's eyes glazed over with fear. *Oh, please don't tell him the truth. It will hurt more than just me.*

Devlin rubbed her arm, silently offering her peace of mind. 'Tracy makes a good executive but a bad executive wife.'

Jessica's tense muscles sagged with relief. She vaguely wondered why he didn't reveal her duplicity. Was she going to pay for it later?

Barry nodded his head in agreement. 'True. About the wife part, that is. Well, I've wasted enough time here. I'm going back to the office. You're going to have a great time explaining all this to the gossips.'

Jessica winced at the thought. She was having enough trouble explaining it to the butler. There was something to be said about hiding in the winery until the furore died down.

'It isn't necessary to explain my actions,' Devlin replied. 'Let them speculate.'

Barry shrugged. 'As long as you don't drag the Parks name in the mud.'

It's been wallowing there long enough, Jessica thought to herself. She pressed her lips together in case she made the fatal mistake of spewing out the words.

Barry took that moment to walk over to Jessica. 'Don't disappoint me.' He poked her in the shoulder.

Jessica bristled. 'Your opinion doesn't matter.' She slapped his hand away and froze. She had never done that before.

Anger rippled through his face. Jessica gritted her teeth,

hating herself for not keeping quiet. She relaxed slightly as Devlin slid his proprietary arm around her waist.

'Thanks for the well wishes, Barry. I'll walk you to your car.' Devlin gave an encouraging squeeze to her hip.

Jessica stood still as she watched Devlin escort her stepfather out of the house. Once she heard the front door swing shut, she lunged for the ultra-slim chrome phone like a drowning swimmer grabbing for a life preserver.

She dialled her sister's phone number and felt a crash of disappointment as the answering machine clicked on. She waited impatiently for the beep. 'Tracy, where the hell are you? I'm stuck in the middle of nowhere with absolutely no money and no way of getting out. Otherwise known as Devlin's home. Get me out of here!'

She ended the call feeling jittery and out of sorts. Where was Tracy? Why wasn't she coming to her rescue? Why wasn't she saving her from this mess? Didn't she realize what was going on? What could Tracy possibly be doing that would prevent her from helping her?

Realization squarely hit Jessica. What if her twin was trapped in yet another one of Devlin's schemes? She could be stuck in that same hotel suite for all she knew. Jessica gasped aloud at the strong possibility.

Oh, I'm a horrible sister. Jessica dropped to the taut rectangular sofa and placed her face in her hands. She had been so concerned about getting away from Devlin and out of the situation, she hadn't even considered how Tracy would get out of her predicament.

OK, it was up to her. Jessica managed to screw up the masquerade and it was her duty to get them all – Tracy, her mother, and herself – out of it. Jessica imagined what her mother must have endured when Barry found out. Jessica raked bent fingers through her hair, accepting the pain because it was easier to deal with than the shame of failing.

She jumped up and stalked over to the windows. First thing firsts, she had to escape from here. She needed to find a way to get her car, cash, and basic necessities. She would get her mother out of Barry's home, find Tracy, and get them all out of Seattle. They'd relocate somewhere far away, safely out of Barry's reach and Devlin's influence.

Jessica swallowed a lump of anxiety. The thought of the men's vengeance was enough to make her knees buckle. Tracy and her mom would have to keep a low profile. That had never been a problem for Jessica, who did a stellar job of being the 'other' twin. They probably would live in poverty, but that was better than prison.

Prison. The word left a sour, bilious taste in her mouth. She would not let that happen to any of her family members. And, if she had anything to do with it, they would not be poor. Her mother definitely wouldn't be able to handle it. But with her computer degree and Tracy's business experience, they might be able to keep their heads above water.

'That was much easier than expected,' Devlin said as he strolled back into the living room.

Jessica jumped and whirled around. 'What?' She had forgotten that Barry was somewhere on the premises.

'Barry left without causing too many problems.' He watched her quietly but with the intensity of a hawk.

'As long as he gets what he wants, he doesn't care about the methods.' That was one trait he shared with her stepfather.

Devlin threaded his hand with hers. 'Now, where were we? I know. I was going to give you the tour. Come with me.'

She reluctantly followed him since she had no choice. It had nothing to do with her pulse skipping from his touch. 'Where are we going?'

'I'm showing you around the house. We'll start upstairs.' He quickly led her up the grand staircase.

'This is a very odd way to conduct a house tour,' she muttered as they took the steps two at a time. She had a very good idea what his plan was, but Jessica didn't stop him.

'If Barry hadn't interrupted, we would have already made our way up here.' He ushered her into the master bedroom suite. The high ceilings and large windows added to the stark, modern style. The sleek dark furnishings and stunning minimal artwork were boldly masculine. The gold-and-green bed coverings mirrored the landscape displayed through the windows, but it also made Jessica feel like she had stumbled into a part of the wilderness. That did very little to calm her runaway nerves.

She cleared her throat. 'You know, I'm surprised Tracy wasn't waiting for us at your doorstep. I'm sure she'll be dropping by soon.'

'Mmm.' He reached out and lifted her chin with his finger. Her eyes met his. '*Our* doorstep.'

Jessica ignored the correction. She knew he was sidestepping the issue. 'What have you done with her?'

Devlin chuckled. 'You make it sound like I'm a member of a crime syndicate.' He stroked the underside of her chin.

His touch stirred her newly awakened senses. 'Are you still "detaining" my sister?' she asked sarcastically.

'Yes. But it's for her own good.' He didn't show any interest in the topic. Devlin was too interested in gaining a response from the light, mesmerizing touch.

Jessica made a face. 'Of all the macho, ridiculous…'

Devlin placed a silencing finger against her lips. Jessica pursed her lips against his skin without thinking. Devlin's eyes blazed as he said, 'I'm keeping her out of firing range of Barry.'

Jessica backed away. 'She can handle herself.'

He dropped his hand. 'Not when Barry finds out why Tracy was out of town.' His eyes swiftly darkened.

The blood drained from Jessica's face. 'You know about that?' Who told? She knew she hadn't. She prayed she didn't drop any clues unintentionally.

'I make it my business to keep informed.'

'When did you find out?' Jessica gnawed on her bottom lip. If she were the one who messed up, she would never forgive herself.

He scowled. 'It's not important.'

'It is to me,' she insisted. 'When did you find out? How long have you known?'

'From the beginning.' Devlin sighed with irritation. 'Since the wedding rehearsal.'

'Aha!' She pointed her finger in front of his face. 'And you tried to feed me all the mumbo-jumbo about my blue eyes.'

Devlin snagged her hand in his fist with lightning speed. 'I knew it was you,' he replied in a withering tone. 'But when I found out about Tracy's negotiation attempts, I knew *why* it was you.'

'If you say so.' Jessica arched her eyebrows, mimicking Devlin's superior expression. She frowned as she considered his words. '"Attempts"?' she said. 'I take it she didn't get the programmer.'

Devlin paused. 'No, she didn't.'

Jessica grew silent. The masquerade was all for nothing. She had fallen into a trap and had nothing to show for it.

There was something peculiar about Devlin's pause. What was he hiding? 'Did you have something to do with that?'

'Yes.' He showed no regret or remorse for interfering in Tracy's plans. It was business as usual for him.

How did the man do it? He was all seeing, all knowing. It

was almost inhuman. 'Next you'll tell me you had something to do with Tracy's plane delay.'

Devlin smiled. He brought her hand to his mouth. His lips tantalised the fragile skin of her wrist. Her pulse leapt.

Jessica hesitated. Did he have the influence to delay Tracy's plane? No…that was ludicrous. 'When are you going to release Tracy?'

'She's free to go,' he murmured against her hand. 'But she knows it's a smart move to stay under my protection for just a little while longer.'

She didn't like the sound of that. It gave the impression that something ominous was about to happen. 'Why are you protecting her?'

Devlin trailed kisses along the lifeline of her palm. 'I have my reasons.'

Jessica frowned. 'That's all you are going to tell me?'

'It's business. And you've told me plenty of times that you don't understand business.' His tongue flicked her hand.

Jessica tried to pull away as desire licked her veins. 'What are you doing?' She hated the huskiness of her voice.

His smile was decidedly wicked. 'Foreplay.'

Heat exploded in her chest. She bestowed a discouraging look. 'And you're telling me this because…?'

'I go back to work tomorrow. Our official honeymoon ends tonight. Let's make the most of it.'

'Believe me, we aren't obligated to celebrate the honeymoon. We've already consummated the marriage.' She turned pink remembering it.

Devlin smiled and moved closer. 'Don't make this anything more than what it is,' he suggested in a low voice.

She didn't fight him as he captured her waist with his hands. 'What is it?' She was keenly interested in his view of their strange relationship.

'I want you.' He shrugged. 'You want me.'

Disappointment crashed heavily on top of her hopeful heart. 'Unfortunately, that's all it is.' *I need more than that. I want more.*

'It didn't pose a problem last night,' he reminded her gently. He curled her closer to him. The heat of his body enveloped her.

She straightened her shoulders and gave him a haughty stare. 'I was fulfilling an obligation.' Her voice sounded breathy even to her own ears, ruining the snooty effect.

'What about fulfilling your wifely duties?' he countered. He lowered his head and playfully nipped her ear.

Jessica blinked rapidly as she belatedly realized the verbal trap she'd stepped into. 'This isn't a real marriage. Why should I act like a real wife?'

'It's real,' he murmured in her ear. The warning tone could not be mistaken. 'I have the documents to prove it.' He probed her ear with his tongue.

Her breath hitched in her throat. She leaned into and then curled away from him. 'You know what I mean.'

Devlin circled the tip of his tongue along the edge of her ear. 'I think it's in our best interest if we try to make the best of the situation.'

'You mean pretend?' Jessica shook her head. She had had enough pretending to last her a lifetime.

'I mean, accepting that we are a married couple and not enemies.'

She would like to live in a home that wasn't a re-enactment of the Cold War. She had had enough of that during her childhood. 'It would make the divorce more amicable.'

Devlin paused his sensual exploration. 'I'm not thinking that far,' he said tersely.

'But this marriage…'

Devlin silenced her with a kiss. 'Hush,' he ordered in a

husky voice. 'Stop worrying and enjoy the moment.'

He kissed her again, surging his tongue through her parted lips. Their tongues thrust and parried and Jessica found the silent duel extremely erotic.

When it felt like her lungs were about to burst, Devlin pulled back. His chest heaved as he gulped in air. His eyes gleamed with passion.

He leaned forward and Jessica waited impatiently for his next kiss. She blinked in surprise as Devlin grabbed the hem of his shirt and pulled it over his head. Her eyes widened at the impressive expanse of his tanned chest. But if he thought she would respond in kind, then Devlin had another thought coming.

She took a step back and knocked her leg against the corner of the bed. Jessica almost lost her balance. Her arms cut through the air like a crazy windmill, but she righted herself before collapsing on the mattress, hitting the sharp edge of the footboard with her leg again.

She grimaced in pain. 'Ouch!' Jessica hopped on one foot as the smarting throb forked through her leg.

'Are you OK?' Devlin reached her. 'Here, let me see it.'

'No, no. I'm fine.' She tried to hide her leg from his intense gaze. 'I can manage,' she said through gritted teeth.

'I'm sure you can, but unless you have X-ray vision,' he added dryly, 'it's best for me to look.'

Devlin took her by the shoulders and sat her down on the bed with an insistent hand. She scooted down the mattress until she was perched on the very edge. Jessica felt very gauche for running into the furniture!

He crouched down in front of her and slipped off her shoe. Her feet tingled as he cupped the ticklish arch of her sole. She tried to pull away, unwilling to show him just how ticklish her feet were. He easily held onto her, his large hand looking very powerful as it palmed her heel.

He tossed the shoe aside and took off her other shoe. 'What do you think you're doing?' she demanded.

'You shoe is going to get in the way.' He cupped her other foot. His thumb slid between her heel to her toes. The teasing touch made her want to shriek. The stimulation was intense, on the brink from pleasure to pain. She tried to kick out of his grasp. No such luck.

'Both of my shoes are in the way?' Her challenging tone was supposed to keep him in line but it only seemed to bring out his playfulness.

Devlin flashed her a sly grin. 'I thought you might feel funny wearing only one shoe.'

'Uh-huh,' she responded sarcastically. 'How thoughtful of you.' She flinched as Devlin's long finger brushed against her bare ankle and dipped under her jeans.

'Devlin,' she warned.

'Is this where it hurts?' he asked innocently. He gently thumbed the grazed skin.

'Yes.' She bit her inner lip as his fingers fanned around her calf, brushing against the back of her knee. If he knew how ticklish she was there, he would zoom in to the area. She was sure of it.

'I'll rub it for you,' he offered. She took it as a threat and Jessica tried to shake him off. 'No, you don't need to.'

'I insist.' He massaged the bruised skin with a tenderness that Jessica didn't think he was capable of. He touched the back of her knee with infinite lightness. It didn't quite tickle, but it made her blood dance in her veins. She wanted to shake her leg like a dog that was getting a good scratch behind his ear.

The light muscle play of his shoulders fascinated Jessica. Without his shirt, Devlin looked primitive and blatantly male. Yet he knelt down in front of her and rubbed her sore leg.

As he massaged the injured spot with the pad of his thumb, Jessica winced. Devlin saw her pained response. 'Take off your jeans, Jess.'

'No way.' There was absolutely no way she was going to take her clothes off in front of him like a stripper. So what if he'd already seen her naked. So what if he already knew her body intimately. There were certain things she wasn't brazen enough to do in full daylight.

Impatience flitted across Devlin's austere features. 'I can't see where you're hurt.'

She scooted to the side. 'You know, it's not that big of a deal. I'll live.'

His hands bracketed her hips, barring her from sliding off the bed. 'Do it.'

Jessica folded her arms across her chest. 'No,' she answered stubbornly.

'I understand that you're still a shy virgin in such situations, but I think you're being ridiculous.'

'What is your problem with shy virgins?' She glared at him. 'I'll have you know that in some cultures, virgins – especially the shy ones – are revered. Even sought after.'

Devlin rolled his eyes heavenwards. 'Spare me the lecture and take off your jeans.'

'No.'

'Take them off before I do it for you. And I should warn you that my way is much, much slower.' His smile grew wider and he looked forward to the prospect.

With sharp, fierce movements, Jessica unsnapped her jeans. She lowered the zipper with such a vicious tug that the metal shrieked against metal. She met Devlin's gaze and glared back as she shucked the denim off her legs.

Devlin grabbed the tough fabric pooling at her bare feet and yanked it away. Jessica fought the urge to cross her legs. It would reveal too much of her discomfort.

His fingers softly roamed her bare leg. Jessica gritted her back teeth at the unsettling touch. 'Are you about through?'

Devlin didn't seem to be listening. 'Yeah, you seem to have banged your leg pretty good there. The skin isn't broken, but you're going to have a nasty bruise.'

'That's fine.' Jessica's mouth set in a disinterested line as she purposefully looked out the window. 'I'll show it off to my friends as a souvenir from my honeymoon.'

A chuckle erupted from Devlin's throat. 'They'll be so disappointed for you. I should give you something else to display.' His wicked smile made Jessica wonder if he planned to cover her body in love bites.

'Don't bother.' She tried to shake off his grasp as Devlin leaned down and brushed a kiss against her chafed skin. It was as soft as a butterfly's wing.

Her lips parted open in surprise as he continued to gently kiss the reddened spot. How was it that the lightest touch seemed to liquefy her bones but, if he had pressed hard kisses on her, her legs would have become rigid?

Did he know how his touch affected her? Most likely. A field of goosebumps blossomed across her skin.

Devlin's gentle mouth grazed against the fragile skin at the back of her knee. She pressed her lips tightly as pleasure zipped across her thigh. His warm breath teased the sensitive skin to the point where she wanted him to press his mouth firmly against her.

He continued his quest along her leg. Jessica's scrape diminished into a low insistent throb. She was too intent on the image of Devlin's dark head trailing along her pale leg.

Devlin's fingers stroked her thigh as he placed gentle kisses above her knee. Her muscles quaked imperceptibly as his fingertips meandered along her soft flesh, creating circular, invisible designs.

His fingers brushed against the lace edge of her panties.

Jessica stiffened as the teasing touch inflamed her senses. Sharp cravings attacked the juncture between her thighs. The pulsating need became so relentless that the next time his fingertips danced along the edge, she didn't back away. She didn't tense. Jessica's body softened, silently welcoming his touch.

Devlin kissed along her inner thigh. The intimate position alarmed and enthralled Jessica. He was too close, yet he wasn't close enough. She was suspended between anxiety and anticipation.

The piercing need was unforgiving. Devlin seemed to know exactly how she felt and she shuddered in relief as he cupped her sex.

His palm pressed her softness and she rocked against the hardness he offered. The temporary reprieve was sinfully sweet. Pleasure rippled from her pelvis and shimmered through her legs.

Jessica tried to bite back her moan, and was almost successful until he stroked her through her lace panties. 'Devlin!' she gasped, buckling forward from the exquisite touch.

Devlin raised his head from her thigh. His slumberous eyes and swollen mouth couldn't detract from the sharp lust stamped on his face. 'Lie down.'

She didn't offer any resistance. She lay down on the bed, offering Devlin free rein of her body for immeasurable pleasure in return. Her breath hitched in her throat as he stoked the damp fire between her thighs. Jessica's eyelids fluttered down as the wondrous sensations swept her away.

Raising her arms above her head, Jessica stretched her body. It was either move every muscle to alleviate the building pressure or explode. When Devlin toyed with the waistband of her panties, she raised her bottom off the bed so he could remove the interfering barrier.

When his mouth replaced his hand, Jessica bolted up. 'Devlin!' she shrieked, scandalized. She gripped his dark hair in her fists and tried to move him away. 'What are you doing?'

He looked up and his eyes danced wickedly. 'Trust me.'

The position was too intimate, too much. 'Devlin, you can't!'

Devlin responded with a soft flick of his tongue.

Jessica's entire body threatened to splinter. Her nails clawed his scalp. 'Oh my…' Her breath disintegrated as Devlin continued the sensual onslaught.

Whether it was the audacious touch or Devlin's single-minded determination to give her pleasure, Jessica discovered the intimacy addictive. Rather than pushing him away, she crept closer to the source of the beautiful intensity. Her legs hooked over Devlin's shoulders and she pressed him closer, desperate to experience all he had to offer.

The climax hit her by surprise. It didn't grow and mushroom until she felt like she would splinter into a thousand pieces. It flashed through her like a blinding light, robbing her of all thought and sense for an infinitesimal moment. Her body clenched as the sensual energy stole her breath.

She gave a high, keening cry that seemed to go on and on until she sagged in relief. Jessica crumbled to the bed, her muscles pulsing and her heart pounding. Devlin crawled the length of her body and she silently welcomed his heat.

'Open up for me,' he demanded, parting her legs with his hands. She did as he commanded. When she felt his hard arousal brushing against her tender thighs, her spent passion flared to full life.

Tilting her hips to accept him fully, she still gasped as he sheathed her to the hilt. Her hips weaved and writhed like a belly dancer as she followed her body's instinct. She saw

Devlin wince from the extreme pleasure. He gripped her hips with rough hands and thrust in to her.

To her utter amazement, she felt the coiling pressure deep in her womb once again. Only this time, the swirling force was more intense. Hotter. More powerful. There was no agonising rise to the peak. She zoomed over the edge as Devlin pulsed inside her. She heard Devlin's shout of pleasure, but her senses were still flying as Devlin cradled her close to him.

As her body started to shut down and exhaustion set it, Devlin's hand crept to where they were intimately joined. He pressed his thumb against the secretive bud. Her overtaxed senses bloomed into life, eager for more. Although Jessica knew she would regret it, she softened under his touch and waited to see what else Devlin had in store for her.

The brisk knock on the door stirred her as she emerged from a sound sleep. She blinked her eyes open and frowned. This was not her bedroom!

'Come in,' Devlin called out, startling Jessica. She suddenly realized she was in Devlin's bedroom. In his bed. Naked! The memories of the night before came flooding back as well. She burrowed deeper under the quilt, pretending to be asleep as Rodgers entered the room with a breakfast tray.

'Thanks, Rodgers,' Devlin said as he accepted the china-laden tray. 'I'll take it from here.' He closed the door behind the butler.

'You can stop pretending, Jess,' Devlin said as he walked to the bed. 'He's gone.'

She wanted to continue faking sleep. It gave her the illusion of safety. But Devlin would be the kind of guy to strip the bedcovers from her.

Jessica squinted in the morning light and stretched. She winced. Her muscles were sore and tender. She struggled to get up, wrapping the crumpled bed sheets around her slender frame.

Devlin smiled knowingly as he placed the breakfast tray on top of her lap. 'Don't get used to this routine.' He indicated the coffee and toast. 'After last night, I knew you would need your rest.'

She glared at his wolfish grin. 'Gee, you're all heart. Had you used the same consideration last night, my muscles wouldn't be screaming for mercy.'

'Aw, but you weren't screaming for mercy either, Jess.' A corner of his smile turned up. 'You were screaming, but I think the words were "Oh"…'

She held her hand up to stop him, her face blushing neon pink. 'Thank you for the replay, but that's quite enough.'

'If it makes you happy, I would gladly kiss it better.'

'Don't you have to go to work? Soon?'

He chuckled. 'Yes.' Deciding he had rattled her enough, Devlin walked to the mirror and put on a blue tie that perfectly matched his shirt.

'Probably be back late, huh?' Jessica poured a cup from the fine china pot, inhaling the fragrant brew. 'I'm sure the wedding stuff set you back.'

He looked at her through the mirror's reflection as he flipped one end of the tie around the other. 'Trying to get rid of me?'

What was your first clue? 'No, no, of course not. I'm…just trying to figure out the daily schedule around here.'

'And what are your plans for today?' He tightened the knot close to his collar.

'My, that sounded very husbandly.'

'I am your husband.' He enunciated each word.

Not for long. She was going to visit the lawyer who advised her stepfather. Jessica hadn't quite figured out all the logistics but if she had to hitchhike her way to Seattle, she'd do it and camp out at the law offices if need be.

Jessica took a sip of the strong blend, ready for a caffeine kick. It was going to be a long, stressful day. Her eyelashes fluttered closed as she rolled the full-bodied taste around her tongue. When she opened her eyes, she found Devlin watching her. His eyes darkened as she enjoyed a simple pleasure.

She set her cup down with a clatter. Jessica looked away, reining in her composure. She had to sound breezy, not scheming. 'I don't have any of my things here. I might pop by my parents' house and get my clothes.'

Devlin slipped on his exquisitely tailored suit jacket. 'No need.'

'Are you kidding me? I can't go around wearing nothing but a bed sheet.' She tugged at the silk fabric.

His eyes lit with a devilish glow and Jessica knew he was running through the infinite possibilities.

Her mouth twisted with impatience. 'I'm serious, Devlin.'

'Your clothes are for a college student,' he explained, straightening his shirt cuffs. 'Not an executive wife.'

Dread weighed heavily on her stomach. She did not want to be an executive wife. That was one of the reasons she had studied for a college degree. She watched as her mother lived through Barry's failures and successes but whatever Lorraine Parks contributed to the projects, it was never appreciated or recognized.

Jessica knew she couldn't live like that. She would go quietly and completely mad. 'I don't want to be an executive wife,' she said, crumbling the corner of her perfectly browned toast with agitated fingers.

'What's so difficult about hosting a few dinner parties?' Devlin asked. 'Or going on business trips with me?'

He didn't understand. And she didn't think it was worth complaining about since she would have the shortest executive wife career in history. 'Nothing,' she muttered, grinding the fragment of toast into dust.

'You'll need some clothes immediately. I know some of my colleagues will want to celebrate our nuptials in style. I'll have my secretary sort something out.'

'Wouldn't it be easier for me to go and pick the clothes out myself?' Jessica couldn't believe she had said that. She did not enjoy shopping but if this was the only way to get out of the house, she would act simply thrilled about the prospect.

'Sounds inconvenient.'

No kidding. She preferred the 'point and click' method on her computer, usually choosing one-size-fits-all styles. 'What else do I have to do today? I guess I could call around and find Tracy. She'll probably be at the office.'

Devlin paused. 'She'll undoubtedly be busy today. You know, changes in management.'

'I can't imagine it throwing the entire day out of whack.' She made a face at the thought. 'Unless you're planning a coup, which would be very unwise on your first day of the job.'

Devlin's smile was pure sin. 'Don't worry about business. I have it all under control, and I'll have a driver take you to the shops.'

Jessica had an awful feeling that the driver would be watching her more than the road. He would probably be built like a football player, run like a track star, and carry a gun – basically designed to interfere with her escape plans.

'I'm sure everyone will be busy and I really don't want to be a bother. I can drive the car myself.'

Devlin gave her a do-you-think-I'm-stupid look. 'I don't think so.' He walked over to her.

'Why not?'

'You don't have your driver's license with you.' He leaned forward and grasped the headboard, barricading her in.

Jessica wanted to growl with frustration. 'I'll dash over to my mom's house and pick it up.' She snapped her fingers. 'Problem solved.'

'Driving without your license is illegal,' Devlin asked mockingly. 'I wouldn't want you to get caught *breaking the law.*'

Jessica's eyes narrowed at the implied reminder. She knew perfectly well that if she were pulled over without her actual license, it would only require a court date. And Devlin knew that too.

'I'll be happy to have a driver at my beck and call,' she said rigidly, knowing that she was supposed to sit tight and enjoy the view of her gilded cage, or her fraud would be revealed. 'How very thoughtful of you.'

Devlin chuckled as triumph glittered in his eyes. 'My pleasure. Until tonight, Jess.'

He bent to kiss her. She quickly offered her cheek. The movement reminded her of something. A collage of images flickered through her mind. *Oh no, I've become my mother!*

chapter eight

Her bodyguard-driver-babysitter turned out to a woman. A fit and able woman who could take her down easily. Jessica's vision of losing her shadow in a public restroom evaporated instantly.

'Anywhere else, Mrs Hunter?' the driver asked, placing a bursting shopping bag in the last available space.

Jessica cringed at the title. She had asked the woman to use her first name. That did not go over well, the employee claiming that Mr Hunter would not approve. Jessica got the feeling that every action and thought would be subject to *Mr Hunter's* approval.

Like the new clothes, for example. Knowing the key words to her new wardrobe were 'appropriate' and 'elegant', she had spent the entire morning with an overly enthusiastic personal shopper. The vineyard's vehicle was now stuffed with the entire spring collection of a top-flight couterier. Jessica had also managed to buy out most of the glamorous shoes and handbag inventory.

The personal shopper wanted to be very thorough and had selected every imaginable lingerie style from bustiers to teddies to babydolls from an exclusive French label. Jessica didn't really care about the type of silk or the quality of lace. She just knew she *wasn't* going to model any of these for Devlin, no matter how much his eyes darkened. She shook the idea aside as her skin prickled.

Jessica put a major dent in Devlin's charge account, but she found no satisfaction in the petty justice. She was too busy looking for an escape route. She needed to get to the law offices before they closed.

The woman's mobile phone buzzed on her hip. She unclipped it from her jeans and turned it on. 'Hello? Oh, yes, sir, we're still shopping. No sir…no sir…'

Jessica idly listened to one-half of the conversation. She knew it was Devlin demanding a step-by-step account of her day. Was he asking if she was 'lost' for a few minutes or had made a mad dash for freedom?

His attitude bothered her – a lot. Should she expect these random phone calls throughout the day? Was this possessiveness a taste of what she would suffer until she got divorced?

The law offices were beckoning at her full force.

'For you, Mrs Hunter.' The woman offered the phone. Jessica smiled and politely thanked the woman, suppressing the urge to smash the phone on the garage forecourt and run it over with the vehicle for good measure.

'Hello?' she said automatically. She wasn't going to act like the blushing bride for the driver's benefit.

'Good afternoon, Mrs Hunter.' He savoured the title. 'How's your day so far?'

'Fine,' she answered dully. 'And yours?'

'Eventful,' he said with unusual care. 'Did you get a dinner dress?'

'"Yes, why? Are we going somewhere tonight?" Ugh! Her first business dinner. Nothing like a baptism of fire to complete her day. Good thing she wasn't going to be around to fully enjoy it!

'Mm-hm. Our patio overlooking the garden – it beats any city restaurant.' It wasn't pride that rippled from his words, more like the anticipation of a new groom looking forward to spending a quiet evening with his wife.

Jessica frowned at the ridiculous notion. If he thought he could romance her into submissiveness, he had another thought coming. 'Are we having guests?'

'No. Everyone except your family realizes that a honeymooning couple value their privacy.'

Jessica chose to ignore that. Her family was only showing their concern. 'I have to dress up for dinner?'

'Would you prefer dining in the bed sheet again?' Amusement coloured his voice. 'It can be arranged.'

'Very funny.' The man was developing a fetish with the bed sheet! 'Don't you have some work to do?'

'Yes, but tormenting you is much more fun,' he said. The seductive tone tingled her spine. She straightened her shoulders, warding it off.

'I'm hanging up now,' she threatened briskly. He was wasting her precious time.

Devlin chuckled. 'See you soon, Jess.'

Jessica clicked the phone off and rubbed her forehead with tense fingers. She only had a few hours. Could she get everything done? Probably not.

'That's the last of it.' The driver slammed the door. 'Are you OK?'

'I'll be fine.' She handed over the phone. 'Just a nagging headache.' *And its name is Devlin.*

'I don't think I have anything for that. I can swing by the chemist,' she offered.

'No, no…' She fumbled into silence as an escape plan formed in her mind. There was a chemist in the downtown area, just a few blocks away from the law offices.

'Mrs Hunter?' The driver's forehead crinkled with worry.

'Oh, sorry.' Jessica formed a strained smile. 'You know, maybe we should make a stop at the pharmacy.'

Jessica leaned against the doorbell of her mother's house. *I'll be safe once I get inside. Once I close the door and bolt it.* If Devlin pursued her, she'd be protected for the moment until Barry got home. To hell with business relations. Her future was at stake!

Too bad that moronic lawyer didn't understand that. He looked at her from above his half-glasses and told her not to worry her 'pretty little head'. His patronising attitude became downright insulting when she mentioned the pre-nuptial agreement she had signed but couldn't relay any of the information. She finally tuned him out when he peppered his lecture with lovely little quotes about marrying in haste and repenting in leisure.

No wonder that eerie little man was Barry's lawyer. The two belonged together. Her visit to the law offices was a waste of time. She could have been packing, or searching through the phone book for a competent attorney.

At least she had got away from the driver. By the time they had parked at the pharmacy, Jessica's fictional migraine had the same pain level as a brain tumour. Her acting skills weren't great despite the practice over the weekend, but it seemed to convince the driver, leaving Jessica in the car and running into the pharmacy.

The moment the driver went inside, Jessica jumped into action. She scrawled a note, giving a vague reference of seeing a friend. She wasn't exactly sure what she wrote – she just had to get out of there quickly.

She figured that would give her a few hours' head start. No one would think too much of her disappearance. Once they did, they would be combing the Seattle neighbourhoods while she was on her way to Canada. Or Mexico. Maybe Hawaii! She hadn't figured that part of the plan out yet.

The front door swung open. 'Jessica!' Relief wreathed Lorraine Parks' face. 'Where have you been? What is going on?'

'Can't talk now.' Jessica ran into the house, skidding on

the marble floor. 'I have to pack. Can you pay the taxi?'

'Jessica!' Her mother called out as Jessica sprinted out the steps. 'Come back here right now and explain.'

Jessica flew open her bedroom door and dove for her bed. *Ahh. I'm home*. She paused for a moment, squirming around to get comfortable. *Well, it doesn't matter*, she decided as she bounced up on to the floor, making a beeline for her wardrobes. She grabbed her suitcase and put it on her bed.

Her mother appeared at the door, somewhat breathless. 'Jessica Ann Parks, what is going on?'

Jessica didn't even know where to start. 'It turns out that Devlin knew all along that I was pretending to be Tracy.' She swiped the hangers off the clothing rod.

'Oh, no.' Lorraine's shoulders sagged with defeat. She clumsily perched herself on the bed. 'Well, where have you been?'

She paused, her arms overflowing with clothes. 'With Devlin.' She dumped the armload into an open suitcase. This was going to be more difficult to explain.

'I don't understand. Why?'

Jessica took a deep breath. 'Because Devlin and I flew down to Las Vegas and got married.' She whirled to the chest of drawers.

'What!' Lorraine yelled, causing Jessica to flinch. Her ladylike mother never raised her voice. 'Devlin knew you weren't Tracy and still married you?'

'The contract's stipulation was to marry a Parks,' Jessica explained, pulling out drawers and shaking the contents into her suitcase. 'It didn't matter who.'

'That doesn't make sense.' Confusion suffused her mother's voice as she tried to understand Devlin's motives. 'Why didn't he take Tracy to Vegas?'

'I don't know.' Jessica paused from her packing. 'By the way, where is Tracy?'

'I haven't a clue. All this time, I couldn't figure out where you were. I thought Tracy was with Devlin on their honeymoon. Maybe she's still in New York.'

Jessica shook her head. 'No. Devlin and Nicholas cornered her in the hotel on the wedding day. I haven't heard or seen her since.'

Her mother's complexion turned ghostly white. 'Oh, my God.' She placed a shaky hand to her throat.

'Don't worry, Mom. Knowing Tracy, she's probably at work. I didn't get a chance to try her office number.'

'I'll do that right now.' Lorraine Parks paused. 'Are you OK, Jessica?'

'I'm fine,' she said automatically. 'I'm just running away. You're coming with me. So is Tracy.'

'Run away?' Her mother paused, searching for the right words. 'Why would you want to do that?'

Jessica gawked. Was her mother serious? 'I didn't want to get married in the first place and Devlin isn't going to release me from the marriage until he's good and ready. Therefore, I'm running away.' She stepped into her adjoining bathroom and scooped up her toiletries.

'Jessica, let's take a moment and consider this.' Her mother spoke with exaggerated patience. It set Jessica's teeth on edge.

'What is there to consider?' Jessica returned to the bedroom.

'Is Devlin cruel? Abusive?' Lorraine asked reluctantly. She obviously didn't want to make a decision if the answer turned out to be affirmative.

Jessica was offended that her mother would even think of the possibility. Devlin did not demonstrate his power through might. 'No, Mom, but that's not the point.' She dumped more stuff into the open bags.

'I wouldn't do anything hasty,' her mother advised. She

stood up, rubbing her arms. 'Wait to see how the marriage works.'

'Wait?' Jessica didn't expect this answer. She had hoped her mother would say, 'Get out as fast as you can...let me help you'.

'Wait for how long?'

'Why are you so hung up on a timetable?' Lorraine chewed on a manicured nail. 'It's not like you had any definite future plans.'

Anger flared inside Jessica. 'Are you saying I should live with a man I hardly know? Just accept the fact that I'm married? You, who just informed me two days ago about the horrors of an arranged marriage?'

'But that's different. I walked into the marriage as an unequal. Barry used my mistake to get what he wanted.'

'How do you think Devlin got me to agree to the marriage?' Jessica whispered fiercely. 'It was either marriage or he would expose the fraud. And he would expose Tracy's and your involvement.'

'Oh dear.' Her mother gnawed on her bottom lip. 'I didn't realize Barry and Devlin are so alike.'

Jessica wanted to tear that statement apart. Devlin was nothing like Barry. Devlin could show tenderness, thoughtfulness.

What am I doing? Defending Devlin? How insane. She didn't want to think about it, and talking to her mother wasn't helping any.

'OK, I'm all packed. Let me help you.' She knew that it had been a good idea not to unpack her boxes when she returned from college. Jessica gave herself a part on the back for her foresight.

'Help me pack? For what? Where am I going?'

The doorbell rang. Jessica ignored it and hoped her mother would do the same. The older woman had a tendency to leave the room when she didn't like the discussion. 'We're running away.'

'No, Jessica.' Her mother tried to sound firm, but her voice shook. 'It would make everything worse.'

'Come on, Mom. You know it's the best way. It's the *only* way!'

'No, Jessica. You are going back to Devlin. You have to fulfil your end of the bargain.'

'For how long, Mom? A decade? Maybe two?'

'For how ever long it takes.' Lorraine paced the floor. She gave a sideways glance. 'I shouldn't have allowed the switch.'

Jessica hands clenched the thick post on her bed. Guilt hit her squarely in the chest. 'I agreed to it, Mom. Remember?'

'And we thought you could pull it off. Now everything is ruined. Worse, we must keep in Devlin's good graces.'

'I don't want to be. I want to be as far away from him as possible. Come on, Mom, before its too late.'

'Go back to Devlin Hunter. I can't keep you here and I can't help you run away.' She looked away, unable to make eye contact. 'If Devlin thinks I helped you escape, I will have two men making my life miserable.'

Tears cascaded down Jessica's cheeks. This could not be happening! She came home for help, for support. Not to be shunned and turned away. She hadn't even considered the possibility in her worst nightmares.

Jessica briskly wiped her wet face. 'Thanks for the advice, Mom.' She pulled her largest suitcase across the floor. 'Tracy and I will send you a postcard.'

'Tracy won't join you,' Lorraine predicted sadly. 'Her status is far too important to give up. She's not going to throw it away to help you hide.'

Her mother had a point, but Jessica didn't want to believe it. 'I'll take that under consideration.'

'If she shows any interest in joining forces,' her mother continued, 'it will only be to use you as a weapon. You have power as Devlin's wife. Why not use it?'

'Hello?' Devlin's voice echoed through the entry hall. Jessica dropped her suitcase in surprise. 'Anyone home?'

How did he find her? Or was it just coincidence? She had to hide. Jessica frantically searched her room. Under the bed? No, too obvious.

Her mother hurried to the bedroom door. 'We're up here, Devlin,' she called.

Jessica's head whipped around in horror. 'Mom!'

She raised a placating hand. 'I'm doing this for your own good,' she whispered.

Jessica slowly shook her head. *No, you're doing it for your own good.*

'Hello, Devlin.' Her mother's mouth fell into the familiar polite smile. 'I understand Congratulations are in order.'

Devlin appeared at the bedroom door. He shook Lorraine's hand. 'Thank you, Mrs Parks. I hope you don't mind me intruding. The door was unlocked but no one answered the bell.'

'It's quite all right. You're family now.' Her hands fluttered nervously. 'Anyway, I was just helping Jessica pack her things to take back to your house.'

Devlin stepped into the room and observed the boxes and suitcases. 'You didn't get enough from the shops?' Devlin teased.

Jessica tried to smile in response but it crumbled before it formed.

'And how was the appointment at the psychic healer?' His mouth twitched with amusement. Jessica grimaced. The excuse seemed perfectly reasonable when she wrote it on the back of a sales receipt before escaping.

'What?' Lorraine's gaze darted to Jessica and then back to Devlin.

Devlin turned to his mother-in-law. 'Jessica had a headache. I believe that it was so intense she required a psychic healer.'

Lorraine was at a loss, apparently uncertain what a psychic healer did. 'Oh, well, as you can see…'

'It didn't do much good.' Devlin nodded his head in agreement. 'I had a feeling it wouldn't, which is why I decided to drop by and see if she was OK. Don't worry, Mrs Parks, I'll take her home so she can rest.'

'Splendid idea. Jessica?'

Jessica's mind shut down, offering her a view of the situation as an out-of-body experience. It was the only way she could prevent the raw pain from killing her. She watched herself pick up the suitcase and walk to Devlin's side. She knew she had to return with Devlin. He managed to box her in at every corner, and her mother wasn't willing to tear out a window. 'I'm ready.'

Devlin and Jessica ate their dinner in a private corner of the flower garden. They quietly watched the sun set, enjoying the rose-and-lavender streaks mellowing into a starlit night. The soft summer breeze brought a citrus floral scent while teasing a hidden wind chime.

Although he tried to maintain some trace of charisma and refinement, Devlin's anger simmered. He had done everything to protect Jessica from her family, and yet she would have gladly tossed it all away. She had run to the enemy, thinking that they would protect her. He hoped that she had learned her lesson.

No, that wasn't true. He didn't enjoy watching her gauzy idealism ripped from her eyes to reveal the gritty reality. Devlin understood the unique pain of being sacrificed for a parent's gain.

He regretted not getting to Jessica before she returned to her parents' house. He could have prevented the conversation he had heard in Jessica's old bedroom. Now truth demanded she face reality head-on. She could no longer view life with naïveté. Devlin was already mourning the old Jessica and he could only hope that she had enough inner strength to draw on for the next few days. Devlin couldn't bear the thought of her turning into an embittered, resentful woman. Or worse, a resigned victim of circumstance.

It was too late to stop his plans. It had always been too late. But why had he changed his mind and taken Jessica as his wife? He had quickly learned to care for her, but was it his affection that had influenced his choice? Or did it have more to do with possessing her? And why did he have this twisting sensation in his gut? While his head had listed all the reasons he had to marry Jessica, he had claimed her for the most primal reasons.

Devlin wanted to crush the doubts banging in his mind. He had never listened to them before and he wasn't going to start now. OK, so he may not go about it with honour and heroism, Devlin admitted as he pushed his poached salmon and grilled summer vegetables around his plate, but he knew he was doing the right thing. He would tell Jessica, but he knew she wouldn't believe him. It was better this way.

'The Chardonnay is delicious,' Jessica murmured, the first unsolicited comment since finding her at the Parks' mansion. 'Very crisp.'

Quiet satisfaction seeped through his chest. 'It's from my label.'

Jessica's eyebrows rose with genuine interest. She opened her mouth but was interrupted by the deep gong of the doorbell. 'Are you expecting someone?'

'No. Rodgers will take care of it.' He was confident that the butler wouldn't let anyone intrude on their private meal.

Jessica took another sip of the Chardonnay, almost choking as Tracy blasted into the hushed garden. Her wineglass landed with a thud, tipping over and staining the pristine tablecloth.

Tracy wasn't even looking at her sister. 'Devlin Hunter, I am going to destroy you,' she vowed as she stomped across the brick patio.

Devlin leaned back in his chair and bit back a frustrated oath. Tracy Parks was the last person he wanted to see at the moment.

Tracy might look like Jessica, but very few people took the time to look past the superficial similarities. Jessica was light personified. She radiated with kindness and purity. Her quiet luminosity beckoned Devlin, reaching the darkest corners of his withered soul.

Tracy was harder. Brash and electric. She invaded a room, sucked out all the energy in everyone and gave nothing in return.

And Jessica wondered how he could tell the difference? It boggled the mind that she didn't see it herself. Perhaps his wife refused to see the bad side of the people she loved. Would she ever treat him that way?

Jessica rose from her seat. 'Tracy, what's wrong?'

Tracy didn't spare her a look. 'I got fired today. Me! Fired! I found out that it was Devlin's orders.'

Jessica faced Devlin. 'Is that true?' Her expression wordlessly begged for it to be false.

'Yes.' His mouth settled into a thin line. Whatever he did would make him the bad guy. He had to get used to it.

'Why?' She looked wounded. 'And please don't brush it off as "business".'

Devlin tossed the linen napkin on the table. Dinner was

ruined and the Parks twins weren't going to let him finish. What was it about that family and their way of intruding on his quiet, private life?

'Tracy, that stunt you tried to pull this weekend shows you're disloyal to the company.' He took a drink from his wineglass. 'I had no other option but to terminate your contract.'

Tracy didn't want to listen to his reasons. 'I've given everything to that company,' she yelled. 'Everything!'

'But you tried to usurp me. And failed. I'm hardly going to let you stay in the company so you can have another chance at it.'

Tracy placed her hands on her hips. 'I must pose quite a threat to you if firing me was your first action as CEO,' she sneered.

Jessica grimaced. 'First action?'

Why was it that every action he took to protect him and his was misconstrued in Jessica's eyes? What would it take for her to see him as a hero? 'I protect what is mine.'

Tracy glared at him, hate blemishing her ice-blue eyes. 'And I will destroy what is yours.'

He glanced at Jessica. She was his and he would protect her or die fighting. He returned his steely glare back at Tracy. 'You try to and I will tear you to shreds.'

'That is enough!' Jessica exclaimed, her eyes wide. Her wide eyes looked unnaturally blue against her pale face.

Tracy whirled her attention to her sister. 'Come on, Jessica. We're leaving.'

Damn! Devlin knew his mistake was looking at Jessica. Tracy was shrewd enough to know he wanted Jessica above all else. She would try to take her away. Hit him where it hurt the most.

And Tracy could quite possibly succeed. Devlin wanted to vault over the table and grab hold of Jessica. Instead, he rose from his seat, his body primed for battle.

'Leave?' Jessica repeated, confused. 'What?'

'Come on!' Tracy lurched forward and grabbed Jessica's arm. 'You want to wait around until he gets to you and ruins your life?'

Was Tracy stupid? Did she really think he would allow her to take Jessica away? 'Take your hands off my wife,' he growled.

'Oh, yes,' Tracy looked over her shoulder at him. 'I heard you legalised the marriage. I should have expected that. Why else would you kidnap me in a hotel room for a weekend.'

'Tracy,' Jessica began, 'It wasn't…'

'What did he lord over you to make you agree?' She looked at her sister with disgust. 'Why didn't you show some backbone and refuse?'

Jessica frowned. She stuttered and fumbled over her words. 'Does it matter?'

'Not really. I'll help get you an annulment.' She yanked Jessica's arm. 'I still have some connections. You can stay at my place until it's over.'

'Jessica will be staying here. Her rightful place is as my wife.' He wanted to push Tracy away, but that would be a major tactical error.

'Jessica doesn't want to stay with you. She doesn't want to have anything to do with you. She only pretended to be your bride as a favour to me.'

'Stop it, both of you!' Jessica screamed, wrenching her arm away from Tracy. 'You're acting like two rabid dogs fighting over a bone.'

Tracy and Devlin stopped and stared at her. Devlin had no idea that the argument was pushing his wife to the edge. He thought she was stronger than that. If she couldn't handle a knock-down-drag-out fight among relatives, she certainly wasn't prepared to meet his side of the family!

Jessica visibly swallowed. Devlin watched, his heart in his throat, as she regained her composure. 'I will remain here, Tracy.'

Devlin held himself rigid as his heart began pumping again. He couldn't believe it. She had decided to stay with him. She chose him over his sister. Why?

'Oh, I get it.' Angry red splotches appeared on Tracy's face. 'Stay friendly with the one who has the power.'

Jessica flinched as if she had been slapped. 'That isn't it at all. If that was how I worked, I would have been the biddable daughter to Barry.'

'Then Devlin must be really, really good.' She turned her wintry eyes on him. 'Turned her head with sex, did you?'

'That's enough,' Devlin bit out. He was ready to pick Tracy up by the scruff of her neck and escort her off his property.

'I haven't even begun.'

'Tracy,' Jessica pleaded, 'don't be like this. Can't we talk like rational adults? Please?'

Her sister scoffed at the suggestion. 'Don't bother.' Tracy swung around and marched back into the mansion with dignity.

Jessica went to follow. Devlin wanted to capture her arm, but refrained from doing so. His hands bunched into fists and then relaxed. 'Let her go,' Devlin ordered gently.

Jessica bit her trembling lip. Her eyes glistened with unshed tears. 'She thinks I've betrayed her.'

'She's upset and tried to use you to get back at me,' Devlin said softly. He knew she was blaming him for the sister rift. He might as well get it out in the open rather than let it fester.

Jessica shook her head. A tear clung to her eyelashes. 'That's not it at all.'

He didn't want to argue. They had more important matters to discuss. 'Why did you choose to stay?' He brushed the tear with his knuckle.

She looked away. 'I don't know.'

He hooked his finger under her chin and tilted her face to meet his. She looked so vulnerable. He felt evil for putting her through all of this. 'Did you choose to stay because I can prove your masquerade?'

She hesitated. 'I really don't know.' She ducked her chin, effectively breaking the physical contact.

Hope squeezed his chest. She could have said 'Yes'. She could have said it had influenced her decision. Yet she acted as if his threat had no bearing. He wondered what did and if he would ever find out.

'I hear you went to your attorney today,' Devlin said as casually as he could while tension coiled his body. Jessica frowned at the seeming change of topic.

She looked into his eyes. 'You really do make it your business to know everything, don't you? Did you influence my attorney in any way?'

'No.' Devlin smiled at the thought. 'I take it he gave you an answer that you didn't particularly like.'

'For the time being,' Jessica answered vaguely, 'I will remain married to you.'

'Don't worry. I'll take care of you,' he promised. He threaded his fingers with hers. For a moment her fingers were rigid as she considered her options of pulling away or staying put.

She stayed put. 'When are people going to realize I don't need a babysitter or a guardian? I don't need to be taken care of!'

'Too bad.' He shrugged. 'That's my job as your husband.' He watched her startle over the term 'husband'. He needed to work on that so that when she heard his name, she automatically thought of 'partner' or 'husband', instead of 'monster'.

The next morning, Jessica woke up groggy. She stretched and her foot bumped against a muscular, hair-roughed leg. She squinted against the morning sunshine. Blinking awake she saw Devlin watching her. His hand propped up his head.

Her heart threatened to burst and spark like fireworks. Her tummy flipped as a tenuous joy filled every fibre of her being.

Oh, no. She was falling in love with him! She couldn't be! It was too soon. Too soon? Too crazy. This was Devlin Hunter she was falling for. The last person she should want to love.

'You're frowning.' He smoothed her forehead with his fingers.

'I'm not a morning person,' she mumbled.

'I know. You prefer all-nighters.'

Jessica blushed. She had spent all night uncovering Devlin's fantasies while discovering she had a few of her own. Yet that was something she could boldly explore in the dark. Yawning dramatically, Jessica stretched her arms and tried to ignore his reference.

Devlin lazily caught her wrist. 'There's something about your hands. I can't place it.'

She moved to stuff them under the sheet. Devlin wouldn't let her and scrutinised her nail-bitten fingers. 'What about them?' Jessica finally asked.

'Something missing. Ah, I know. A ring.'

Jessica made a face. 'I'm really sorry about throwing that ring at you. It was uncalled for.' And one of her lowest moments. She was at her most vulnerable and had done little to hide the fact.

'I got your message loud and clear.' He reached over to

his beside table and produced a black box.

'Oh…Devlin. You shouldn't have.' And she really meant it. Wearing a ring when she really wasn't his bride was bad enough. Now she was supposed to wear his ring knowing that she wasn't a full-term wife.

'You are my wife. You wear my ring.' Devlin acted as if it was as simple as that.

Jessica felt wretched about the idea of a ring. She should have kept quiet about it, no matter how much it bothered her. She stared at the box, knowing she had accidentally made it an issue between them.

'Open it,' he said quietly. Tension radiated from him. She didn't know why.

She hesitated and then did as he ordered. She gasped as the brilliant square-cut sapphire dazzled back at her.

'Devlin,' she blinked at the dazzling stone. 'This is too much.'

'Do you like it?'

It was the kind of ring a man gave his soul mate, a lover gave to the woman of his dreams. Didn't Devlin realize that? Didn't he see how inappropriate the ring was, under the circumstances? 'It's beautiful,' she whispered.

'Like your eyes.' Devlin plucked the ring from its black satin bedding and placed it on Jessica's wedding finger. He curled his hand around hers, lifting it to his mouth.

Jessica felt the familiar stirring of desire and need. She looked away, unwilling to show how she felt. She still felt vulnerable.

'I'll get you a matching bracelet next,' he promised, pressing his lips against the tripping pulse in her wrist.

'No, no,' she shook her head. 'That's too much.' She didn't want him to be extravagant with her. She didn't want the presents, not unless there was love behind the meaning.

'Nothing is too much for my wife,' he announced,

capturing both wrists and stretching them above her head. 'Maybe two sapphire bracelets.'

'Devlin,' she warned. He couldn't be serious!

He hovered above her nude figure. She was extremely aware at how her breasts thrust in the air, ready for his mouth. Jessica was almost disappointed when he chose to pay attention to her forehead instead.

He slicked his mouth against her brow. 'Do they make jewelled headbands?'

'No,' she replied adamantly. Where on earth did he expect her to wear all these jewels?

'That's too bad. I will have to get you sapphire combs instead. Maybe a tiara?'

'Absolutely not!' She tried to remain rigid in his dominating embrace. His playfulness was contagious and she wanted too much to make the pillow talk into more than what it was.

His mouth brushed against the bridge of her nose. 'Nose ring?'

Jessica laughed in spite of herself. 'You're kidding me, right?'

Devlin's teasing lips trailed across her cheekbones and rested on her earlobes. 'Definitely earrings. Big sapphires to complement your eyes.'

'I don't wear earrings, remember? It's what got me in trouble.' She tried to infuse some reality. They had to bear in mind how and why they had really got together.

Devlin refused to listen as he nipped her earlobe. 'All the more reason to get you earrings. I'll order them immediately.'

She shook her head, but Devlin continued on, placing a trail of kisses along her collarbone. 'I'll have a necklace designed for you as well. Maybe a choker.' He began to press kisses down her breastbone.'

'Devlin,' she said in a withering tone. 'Unless you plan on designing a chastity belt, I don't see any reason for you to continue.'

'Now there's a thought.' His eyes sparkled. 'And, of course, I will only have the key.'

'Like I would stay still long enough for you to put it on me? Get back up here, Devlin. Believe me, you could not put another piece of jewellery on me.'

'On the contrary,' Devlin murmured against the slope of her breast. 'The body jewellery available today is limitless.' He circled his tongue around her tight nipple, causing Jessica to inhale sharply.

A knock on the bedroom door startled her. Jessica bucked Devlin off her and yanked the crumpled bed sheets up to her chin.

'Go away, Rodgers,' Devlin called out. He tugged the sheets from Jessica and slowly revealed her aroused body as if he were unwrapping a gift.

'I'm sorry to bother you, sir,' the butler said, his voice heavy with apology. 'You have a visitor.'

'At this ungodly hour?' Devlin sounded distracted as he splayed his hand on her abdomen. 'Send them away.'

'It's your mother.'

The transformation of Devlin's face frightened Jessica. It was like he was informed that the Grim Reaper was waiting for him. The twinkle in his amber eyes disappeared and bleakness settled.

'Hell,' he whispered fiercely and bolted out of the bed. 'I'll be right down,' he called out to Rodgers. Devlin stalked into the adjoining bathroom and slammed the door behind him.

Jessica huddled on the bed. She had a premonition that her mother-in-law was going to be trouble.

chapter nine

Carlotta Hunter was not at all what Jessica expected. She was short and petite, dressed in a chic white pantsuit and flirty white heels. Her mousy hair sported an auburn rinse and her discreet cosmetics made it difficult to determine her true age.

But her mother-in-law's face showed a life of disappointments. There was no softness. Faint lines creased around cold green eyes. Her mouth was set in a straight line.

'There you are, Devlin.' Carlotta remained standing at the window. 'You've had me waiting for nearly half-an-hour.' Her voice didn't hold the motherly warmth of a scolding. It was sharp, unforgiving.

'Considering you gave us no forewarning,' Devlin replied carelessly, 'I find it extremely polite.' He made no move to greet his mother and he showed no intention of introducing Jessica.

Carlotta huffed. The cold greeting didn't phase her one bit. 'Since when do you know anything about being polite?'

'I know it's impolite to bully our butler into giving you a guest room,' Devlin replied. The biting tone made Jessica chew her inner lip. 'Or to intrude on a couple's honeymoon.'

'Oh, yes. The honeymoon.' The simple words took on a complex meaning.

Jessica watched the exchange quietly. Obviously, the mother-and-son relationship was strained. But she had been under the impression that Carlotta was enthusiastic about the wedding. Now she wondered why Devlin had misled her.

Carlotta's gazed whipped briefly over Jessica's figure. 'So the two of you did get married.' Her eyes sliced back to Devlin. 'That wasn't the plan.'

Devlin tensed like a warrior reaching for his sword. Jessica quickly went into action to prevent the argument brewing under the surface. Now was as good time as any to shed the damsel-in-distress image.

'No, Mrs Hunter, it wasn't the plan.' Her voice wobbled, but it could be clearly heard. 'Tracy was unable to take part in the agreement. I took her place.' Jessica stepped forward with a shaky smile and offered her hand. 'We haven't been formally introduced. I'm Jessica.'

Devlin's taunt body vibrated with barely-leashed energy. Carlotta's eyebrows rose mockingly. She flashed a glittering, knowing look at Devlin before she took Jessica's proffered hand.

'How charming.' Her tone implicated that she was anything but. Jessica withdrew from Carlotta's limp, disinterested grasp.

Jessica grounded her back teeth, biting off a reply. She would be polite if it killed her. Whether she liked it or not, this was her mother-in-law. Family was family. Anyway, if she could handle Devlin, she could handle anyone.

Devlin cupped her shoulder with his large hand. The physical touch reminded her of his protection. His possessiveness. 'Jessica,' he said, 'would you please excuse us. I'm sure my mother has something to discuss with me. Why else would she have flown in from Australia and descended on us?' Although Devlin spoke to Jessica, his attention was squarely on his mother.

'But I haven't had the chance to get to know my daughter-in-law,' his mother replied with sugary sweetness. Jessica felt the first twinges of an anxiety attack from Carlotta's frosty eyes. 'I'm sure we'll find plenty to discuss.'

'And I'm sure you'll have plenty of opportunity.' He moved forward and curled his fingers around his mother's upper arm. 'We'll be in my study.'

Jessica quietly nodded, watching as Devlin shepherded his mother past the double doors. She caught a brief glimpse of his face as he closed the doors with a determined click. The guarded expression saddened her. She instinctively knew he was guarding *her*. She was a liability to this powerful man.

Why was he trying to protect her from his own mother? She might be rude and able to slice her into strips with a few well-chosen words, but Jessica didn't need protection. She could handle things herself. After all, how difficult could one woman be?

'Can't you get a simple plan straight?' Carlotta fumed as she stalked his book-lined study. Any veneer of civility had melted the moment they were alone. As always.

Devlin sat behind his sleek black desk. He watched as his mother ranted, invading his sanctuary. Her presence poisoned the room. He wondered how long it would take to make the air seem clean and pure again.

'Everything is in place,' Devlin replied, watching his mother with no expression. He leaned back in the chair. 'Calm yourself.'

'Calm myself?' She whirled around, her green eyes wild. 'Calm myself! I have spent over thirty years working towards this moment and my plans are coming apart at the seams!' She marched over to his desk, her slight body ready to explode with anger.

'There was a problem at the wedding and I took care of it.' Devlin rocked back and forth on the chair. 'It required some changes.'

Carlotta slammed her bony fists onto his desk. 'You were

supposed to dump the bride at the altar,' she hissed. 'How difficult could that be? What on earth went wrong?'

Devlin ignored her anger and met her glare with his unconcerned gaze. 'They switched the bride on me. I decided to let them sweat it out by not returning the one they offered.' He hoped Jessica wasn't listening through the keyhole.

Carlotta's eyebrows slanted upwards. 'Is that right?' She straightened, her mind whirring with the new information. 'Of course,' she whispered to herself, 'I should have expected Barry would pull a stunt like that.'

Devlin steepled his fingers together. His mother's tunnel vision made her blind to outside interference. 'What makes you think Barry had something to do with it?'

'Of course he did.' Carlotta angrily swung her arm in the air. 'That kind of double-crossing is just his style. He'll be dropping by soon to gloat of his trickery.'

'Perhaps his daughters learned a few things from him.' Let Carlotta think she's not the only one wanting to destroy Barry. Let her back off and sniff around for danger. Just for a little while longer. It was wishful thinking, but Devlin was desperate. He wanted more time with Jessica. More time when she wouldn't see him as the monster that he was.

'Stepdaughters,' she corrected hotly, her pale face mottling with red splotches. 'Don't forget that. They are his stepdaughters. And they couldn't possibly pull something like this. Especially that little piece of fluff you married.'

'There is more to Jessica than what you see.' His mother would destroy anyone powerless and innocent – because she could! Jessica might be innocent, but her unpredictability gave her power. He needed to play that up, in case she had to protect herself.

Carlotta's skeletal shoulders shook with silent mirth. 'The

girl is scared of her own shadow,' his mother decided. 'At least she's easy to control.'

Devlin murmured an answer. His mother would not understand that even the most innocent could wreak havoc.

'If anything, she's a distraction. She's weighing you down. You should have left the girl at the altar.'

Devlin ignored the words scraping at his heart. That would have been unforgivable. Her family would have destroyed her. 'And then what? Lose my position in the company?'

'You and I both know that position is meaningless. You already have a claim on Parks.'

'That's because we know the truth,' he patiently reminded his mother. 'Barry sees the enemies circling outside. He hasn't found the enemy within his company.'

'Not yet.' Carlotta smiled with grim satisfaction. 'I can't wait.'

Her dark excitement made his bilious stomach burn. 'I'm sure of that.' *The woman has lived for this moment. Nothing else has ever mattered. Nothing!*

Carlotta glared at him. 'No more surprises, is that understood? We can't afford any improvising this late in the game.'

It was amazing that his mother thought she could order him around. He'd allow that misleading image only because it suited his purposes. 'And then what?'

Carlotta frowned, marring her perfectly smooth forehead. 'What are you talking about?'

'Once you get your revenge, then what?' *Had she even looked past that moment? Her life was going to be meaningless without the malicious goal.*

'Then we take over Parks Software Systems. Right where we should be.' She thumped her manicured finger on the smooth surface of his desk.

'Then I wish you luck.' Devlin put down the pen, preparing for the ugly scene that lay ahead. 'I have no interest in heading the company.'

Carlotta's eyes blazed with irritation. 'Fine time telling me that now!' She threw her bejewelled hands in the air.

'This company is your goal. This is your revenge. I am just the weapon. The enforcer.' He had never said those words, but he had felt them since he was a child. It was a fact his mother didn't dispute, which came as no surprise.

'Are you telling me that you are just going to walk away from it all?' Carlotta obviously couldn't comprehend the idea. This had been her mission, her reason for living. It was unfathomable that he didn't want to share it.

'Yes. That is exactly what I intend to do.' He would honour his mother's wishes, fulfil his destiny, and then walk away.

'Have you lost your mind? You're refusing a company worth millions!' she screeched. 'God, where did I go wrong in raising you?'

Devlin chomped down on his tongue, his jaw popping from the violent move. He knew it would be in everyone's best interest not to answer that. Long ago, he had come to terms with his childhood. He had no intention of revisiting it.

'Fine.' Carlotta waved her hands around. 'Be that way. I will enjoy the reward.'

Devlin once again chose to remain silent. His teeth threaten to shatter under the pressure. His opinion didn't matter. He needed to focus and just get the job done.

'And what will you do?' Carlotta asked.

Did she really care? Or was she concerned that he had plans to steal her reward? 'I have some ideas.'

'Don't tell me, you going to play the gentleman farmer and stay on this vineyard.' Carlotta walked to the window and peered out. She shook her head in disgust.

His mother understood him better than he had anticipated. He filed that unsettling fact away for future use. 'The thought had crossed my mind.'

Carlotta snorted. 'Your loss. Perhaps I should get this in writing. I don't want you changing your mind again.'

"Don't worry. I won't.' He could guarantee it.

His mother cast a shrewd glance at his stony expression. 'It should be interesting to see how fast the little wife deserts you once you're no longer in charge of Parks.'

Misery seeped into his bones. He wondered the same thing. He would lose the woman he wanted, needed and loved, because she would find out what he really was. 'It won't take too long,' he answered quietly. 'Jessica is not a country girl.'

Carlotta laughed, the brittle sound irritating his nerves. 'Country has nothing to do with it. She may be a wimp, but she knows a good thing when she sees one. She'll leave you once you relinquish control. I guarantee it.'

Devlin knew better. Jessica would leave him once he revealed his true interest in Parks Software Systems. But that was something Carlotta's cold black heart would never understand.

The woman was a witch, Jessica decided hours later. She had tried to at least be the perfect hostess, if she was doomed to be the unwanted daughter-in-law.

They were in the sitting room, viewing the grand Cascades mountain range and drinking a bracing cup of tea. Jessica never indulged in this pastime. She was a Northwestern girl who preferred a mug of strong coffee. She also preferred receiving her caffeine intake in silence. Jessica was doing her best to ignore pointed, sharp remarks without looking stupid.

'How long are you planning on staying in America, Mrs Hunter?' Jessica asked when there was an uncomfortable lull in the conversation. She took a sip of tea and winced at the bitterness.

'I've only just arrived,' Carlotta replied with a disapproving frown. 'Trying to get rid of me already?'

'No, of course not.' The bid for small talk fell flat on its face, leaving Jessica flustered. She tried to think of a saving reason for her question. 'I thought of…giving a small dinner party here in your honour.'

'How small?' Carlotta's face lit up with interest – the first time she had shown any positive expression since Jessica was stuck with her.

Jessica culled her mind, desperate for inspiration. 'Just a few friends and business associates.' Maybe the entire staff at Parks Software System. She'd make the dinner into a cocktail party and stay far, far away from Carlotta Hunter.

'Why would I be interested in meeting them?' Carlotta asked snidely. 'I should at least be introduced to your family.'

Jessica realized that, but she was very reluctant. Put her relatives in a room with her mother-in-law and the only thing they had in common was their disappointment in her! 'Well, uh, there's my mother and stepfather.'

Carlotta leaned forward in her chair. 'Now that has potential. Anyone else?'

'Yes. And possibly my sister.' She didn't think it was necessary to mention Tracy's refusal to speak to her. Jessica would do her best to get as much reinforcement as possible.

'Hmm,' Carlotta purred. 'Sounds delightful. Perfect, actually.'

Jessica smiled in a vague response and hurriedly sipped the bitter tea. Her mother-in-law's chilling tone frayed at her spine, exposing her sixth sense for trouble. She had a feeling that the dinner party was going to be a test of endurance.

A strange satisfied smile smeared across her mother-in-law's lips. 'We'll have it tomorrow,' Carlotta announced.

Jessica coughed and spluttered, hastily grabbing a snow-white cloth napkin. The temerity of the woman! 'Oh,' she blurted out, wondering how to get out of the party. She couldn't come up with a quick enough reason. 'Well, if my parents don't have plans…'

'They can break them.' She shooed away the excuse with a flick of her wrist. 'Isn't meeting Devlin's relative more important than some boring social function?'

Jessica paused, her mouth hanging open. 'Well,' she finally said, 'I'll see if they are available. I'm sure they would be very interested in meeting you.' And the sooner the better, if it meant Carlotta Hunter would leave shortly thereafter!

'Tell me, Jessica,' his mother said, as she sipped from the fine bone teacup. 'However did you trap Devlin into marrying you?'

Jessica bristled at the term 'trap'. She was the one trapped! Although it hadn't felt that way at times. Jessica pushed the thought aside and answered the question as coolly as possible. 'He needed to marry a Park and I was the only available one in the area.'

'Needed to?' Carlotta's face hardened. 'I wouldn't go that far.'

Jessica wasn't about to split semantics with the woman. Needed to, wanted to, it didn't matter. Sure, Devlin was not a man who needed anyone or anything. He was just impatient to get the CEO position and didn't feel like waiting for Tracy.

'Mrs Hunter, I have no idea how Devlin's mind works.' She flexed her fingers against the cup handle. The last thing she needed was the china breaking in her hand. 'You would have to talk to him to understand his motives.'

Carlotta rolled her eyes theatrically. 'Believe me, I did earlier before he stormed off to work.'

'Talk' was using the term loosely. Even though she couldn't make out the words, Jessica heard Carlotta's yelling and Devlin's occasional barks of anger.

'But you're right about Devlin,' Carlotta continued in a chatty manner that made Jessica inexplicably suspicious. 'No one can pin down how his mind works. Sure, it got him some financial success, but it also made him some enemies.'

Jessica absently nodded, wondering how long teatime actually had to last before she could make an escape. Her first stop would be the kitchen. She would bury the tea tin if it meant no more of that stressful ritual.

'He says one thing and does another. Decides to go into one business and then shoots off to a different one. He's like that in his personal life, too.'

Jessica calmly placed her cup onto the saucer. Exactly what was his mother saying? That Devlin didn't understand the concept of fidelity?

'Oh, I'm sure this sounds harsh coming from his own mother, but Devlin does have a track record of being unfaithful.' Bitterness pinched her well-preserved features. 'But then, most men are like that.'

Anger boiled inside of Jessica. How dare her mother-in-law try to stir up trouble? She had no idea what the reasons behind it were, but Jessica knew she had to stop it immediately.

'You're wrong, Mrs Hunter. Devlin has his own code of honour and he follows it.'

Carlotta chirped with malicious glee. 'Devlin? Honourable?'

The anger threatened to spill over. 'Yes. Honourable. He

might have less than stellar ways of accomplishing his goals, but he does take care of his own.'

'Well, well, well.' Carlotta tilted her head and studied Jessica thoughtfully. 'It appears that the wife Devlin is saddled with is trying to make the arranged marriage into a love match.'

Jessica flinched. Was she that obvious? Did Devlin notice it as well? She shook her head. Now wasn't the time to mull it over. 'You may think what you like, Mrs Hunter. Just don't voice it. Especially if the person is not around to defend himself.'

'Why does Devlin need to defend himself when he has you as his…protector?' She made the word sound like a joke. Like a slur.

Jessica stood up, her body quivering with fury. 'You may enjoy some privileges being Devlin's mother, but maligning him in his own home is not one of them. I will not tolerate it, is that understood?'

'The little woman defending her husband's name,' Carlotta Hunter tsked. 'Isn't that cute?'

Jessica clenched her teeth together. 'Is that understood?' she slowly repeated. She prayed Carlotta would back down. Jessica had no power to enforce her demand.

Carlotta lounged back in her seat and idly studied the pattern of her teacup. 'You do realize that defending Devlin's name is a waste of time.' She looked back at Jessica, her eyes glittering with a sinister energy. 'His family name, that is. He's a bastard, you know.'

Jessica imagined Devlin as a young boy. An unwanted son. A house governed by conditional love, not unlike her own home. 'His circumstance of birth doesn't make a difference to me.' Jessica's voice shook.

'Nor to me,' the familiar masculine voice said at the far corner of the room.

Jessica jerked around and saw Devlin leaning against the doorframe. His casual pose belied the fire spitting from his eyes. She closed her eyes briefly, regretting that he had heard his mother's point of view. He had probably heard it all his life, but it didn't lessen the pain.

'Devlin,' Jessica managed to say. She wanted to walk over and touch him. She wanted to physically show her support. Demonstrate that his illegitimacy didn't bother her the way it bothered his mother.

But Devlin would shirk away from any offer of comfort. He never asked for it, and he certainly didn't want it. Jessica cleared her throat nervously and remained standing where she was. 'We weren't expecting you home so early.'

'Yes, I gathered that.' He shot a meaningful look at his mother, who chose to ignore it. 'Jessica, come into my office now.'

'Go right ahead,' Carlotta offered her permission, oblivious that no one asked for it. 'Jessica needn't entertain me constantly. She has to put together her little dinner party.'

Devlin tensed. 'Dinner party?' The atmosphere immediately crackled.

Jessica quickly explained, not willing to find out Carlotta's spin on it. 'Your mother expressed an interest in meeting my family. We decided to do it tomorrow. Is that OK?'

He looked away, his eyes empty and bleak. 'Yes, of course.' He swivelled on his heel and walked to the room in question. Jessica hurried after him.

'Devlin, I apologise for not mentioning the party sooner,' she said, her low-heeled sandals clopping against the wooden floor as she ran after him. 'I don't even know where I got the idea. I was just talking to your mother and...'

'The get-together had to happen sooner or later,' Devlin

interrupted in a tired voice. He held the office door open for her. 'Might as well get it over with.'

'If you're all right with it, why did you call me into your office?' She didn't appreciate being treated like a wayward schoolgirl.

'To thank you.' The door closed behind him with a thud. 'For defending me.'

Jessica blushed. She had no idea how much he had heard. 'Totally unnecessary, I know.'

'Not to me.' He leaned over and brushed a kiss over her startled, parted lips. 'Such a vigorous defence is quite a novelty for me.'

Her skin burned brighter. 'You don't have to rub it in. I'm sure I looked like a fool.'

'No, not at all. More like an avenging angel.' Devlin dipped his head and kissed her thoroughly.

Heat coursed through Jessica and she melded into his hot embrace. Her hip rubbed against his hard arousal. 'Devlin!'

Devlin ignored her questioning, yet excited, exclamation. He backed up until his legs brushed up against his office chair. He sat down and pulled Jessica on to his lap. She bit back a yelp.

'Devlin, stop this,' she whispered fiercely. She combated his persistent hands. 'Someone might walk in.'

'No one will interrupt me in my office.' He nuzzled the sweet spot on her throat.

'They will if Rodgers is your guard dog,' she pointed out. Her voice was unnaturally gruff as she fought the languorous heat invading her.

'You have my word on it.' He laved her skin with his rough tongue. 'I promise.'

'But…but…' She was running out of excuses, out of reasons to keep her hands to herself and refuse his advances.

'Hush.' His eyes gleamed with desire. 'Why don't you put

those lips to good use and kiss me?' he challenged.

Jessica fell silent. Kiss him? She had never initiated a kiss. And, she realized, she wanted to!

Cupping his angular face with her small hands, she brushed her lips gently against his. Sexual power sizzled in her veins. Emboldened by his sharp intake of breath, she nibbled along the edge of his firm mouth before suckling the full bottom lip.

'Jess…'

'Hush.' She swiped her tongue against the swollen lip. Devlin responded by placing his large hand at the base of her skull and cradling her closer.

Their lips melded, their breaths entwined. Jessica's hands slid into his thick hair. She couldn't voice or declare her love, he wouldn't tolerate that. But she would demonstrate it. She would show him with every kiss and every caress, knowing that he would greedily accept it all.

Jessica slicked her tongue down the column of his throat. The salty taste of his skin was like an aphrodisiac. The earthy, male flavour was uniquely him.

She unbuttoned his collar. 'You dress too formally,' she murmured against the dip of his collarbone.

'Is that right?' he asked lazily. Devlin sounded dazed. She glanced up at him. His eyes were blurry with desire and his face was tight and flushed. The longing expression licked at her rebellious spirit. She grabbed the front of his shirt and tore it open. The buttons popped and danced across the floor.

'Jess.' There was no reprimand or shock tinting his voice. It was more of a warning that her feminine assertiveness would be met with masculine aggression.

'Hmm?' She splayed her hands on his chest. The heated flesh made her bones go limp. She smoothed her hands against the flat nipples. She wondered if he was as sensitive in that area as she.

Jessica rubbed his flat nipples. To her surprise, her breasts felt heavy and full in response. Devlin tensed under her curious hands. She looked at him mischievously through her lowered lashes.

'I'm sorry,' she whispered. 'Did I hurt you?'

'No,' he answered tersely.

Jessica continued teasing his nipples into tight pebbles. Her nipples furled and strained against her thin brassiere and dress. She leaned forward and flicked her tongue on Devlin's brown aureole.

He flinched. Devlin's fingers dug into her scalp. 'Jess, you are playing with fire.'

'No, Devlin, you are.' She gave a husky chuckle. Did that seductive sound just come from her? 'But if you want me to stop, I will.'

'No.' He cleared his throat and purposefully moved his hands to the armrests. 'I'm interested to see how far my chaste wife is willing to go.'

Jessica hid her smile at the challenge. If Devlin thought she would hesitate because of her virginal sensibilities, then he didn't take her overwhelming curiosity and affection into consideration.

She slid off his lap and knelt between his sprawled legs. Jessica covered his bronze chest with soft, slick kisses. She slowly made her way to the dark hair arrowing past his waistband.

Jessica fumbled with his belt buckle, bumping against his hard arousal. His body heat was intense. When she finally undid his belt, Jessica carefully lowered his zipper.

She glanced at Devlin's face. His features were tight and his eyes glittered with need. Jessica's bravado wavered for a moment. She was in unfamiliar territory. What was she doing trying to seduce Devlin?

'Don't stop,' Devlin ordered hoarsely.

Guided by her building need to touch him, Jessica scrunched down his trousers and underwear. Devlin's thick arousal sprang up, eager for attention.

Jessica grasped him with both hands. He pulsed under her fingers. The heat emanating from him was scalding.

Devlin groaned as she gave an experimental squeeze. He tossed his head back. His eyes clenched shut. His knuckles were white as his fingers raked the armrests.

Jessica slid her hand upward, watching the pleasure ripple across Devlin's face. She repeated the action with her other hand. His expression was more intense as he grew thicker beneath her palm.

She awkwardly continued the pattern until she felt confident enough to try the occasional variation. Squeezing harder or softer, at the base or at the tip. Whether he bucked or writhed in response, each movement gave him immense satisfaction.

Jessica wanted to give him more pleasure. She wanted to taste his heat. As he grew thicker, she felt a coil of heat tighten around her pelvis.

She leaned forward and pressed her lips against the tip of his arousal.

Devlin jumped. His hands grabbed her skull and pulled her back.

'Jess, you...'

'Let me, Devlin. Let me put my lips to good use,' she teased. His capitulation was almost immediate. Jessica knew then how much he wanted her mouth on him.

Only she had no idea how to pleasure him. Guided by instinct, she kissed and lapped her tongue around him. Keenly aware of his responses, Jessica quickly learned what touch made his breath hitch in his throat and what made him moan.

His hands tangled in her hair as he rubbed her head in

silent encouragement and approval. His fingers tightened against her scalp when she accepted him between her lips. Devlin reached a new level of tension.

'Jess,' he said urgently. 'Stand up.'

She frowned. What did she do wrong? 'But...'

'Now.'

Jessica stood, her legs shaky like a newborn colt. Devlin reached for her. He pulled her forward until she straddled his hips. Impatiently bunching up her dress, he shoved her lace panties aside and drove into her.

She gasped from the visceral invasion. Jessica clung to his shoulders as she rotated her hips, accepting him fully. His hands clamped her bare hips.

'Yes,' Devlin hissed. He burrowed his head between her breasts. 'That feels so good. Just like that.'

Jessica rocked against him, testing the overwhelming sense of fullness. Each movement licked fire against her flesh. The fire grew bolder and brighter. Hotter and hotter until she rode him with abandon. The chair squeaked and tilted and their raspy breaths and soft moans punctured the thick air.

Devlin trailed his hand to where they were intimately joined. He pressed his thumb against the secret pearl that lay hidden behind her brown curls. The pressure sent her over the sharp edge and into sensual bliss. She arched her back as her muscles contracted around Devlin, setting off a chain reaction.

Jessica met each of Devlin's sharp, choppy thrusts. The tight coil wrapping around her womb spun into ribbons of heat, snaking through her limbs and abdomen. She embraced the brilliant force and hoped Devlin felt it too. She captured his face between her hands and pressed her parted lips against his open mouth.

The kiss shattered his control. Devlin surged into her as

he moaned into her welcoming mouth before sagging in to the office chair. His body continued to pulse as he slumped with exhaustion.

Jessica curled her arms and legs around him. She wasn't ready to give up the exquisite magic, but each moment she held him exposed her vulnerable heart. How could the pure beauty of expressing her love be both a gift and a curse?

As the sensual storm passed, Devlin shifted in the creaking chair, cradling Jessica closer. Their clothes were mussed and bunched. Their chests heaved as sweat gleamed from their reddened skin. As Jessica nestled her face into his neck, Devlin closed his eyes and sighed.

Contentment spread through him. He used to think 'content' meant 'bored' – that it was a weak and fleeting frame of thought.

Now he knew better. He had been so jealous of those whose faces glowed with contentment. His emaciated soul instinctively knew that contentment was more powerful than satisfaction. Stronger than happiness.

Devlin absently stroked Jessica's long, soft hair. What was it about her? She touched him shyly, yet her fingers aroused him faster than the most experienced women he knew. Need clawed his insides as she lapped her soft tongue against his throat. When she circled kisses around his heart, he thought he would splinter.

He was overwhelmed by her affection. He wouldn't fool himself and call it love. He was unlovable, he knew that. Even someone with a sweet spirit like Jessica could not love him. Affection was as good as it would get and he gladly accepted it with both hands.

'We should get up,' Jessica murmured against his neck. She pressed her lips against his sweat-slicked skin. She tried to pass it as an accidental brush but Devlin knew better.

'A few more minutes.' A few more stolen moments of revelling in the soft intimacy. Of breathing in Jessica's purity.

Her power was quiet but incredible. How did she manage to wipe the poisonous atmosphere from this room? How did she encourage hope from his dead soul? Love from his crippled heart?

Did she have the power to cleanse him entirely? To strip away the decay that controlled his life? Teach him to create instead of destroy?

No, she didn't, even if she had wanted to. Jessica would leave him within the week. She would escape from him before he tainted her life. She was strong enough to break away.

It was too late to stop the revenge. Devlin cursed his own weakness. He may have had the power to put it all into place, but it gained momentum on its own. Unfortunately, he didn't have the power to protect her from the revenge – she would get hurt. Knowing that he couldn't save her was quietly killing him.

Devlin gave a shuddering sigh. Jessica stirred and he threaded his fingers through her hair.

It was best to finish what was started. Free himself from the bondage his family had placed on him at birth. Make the world just for one brief moment. Sacrifice his happiness and distance himself from this woman, who deserved more.

The thought alone killed him, but he had to do it. Because he loved her so intensely, Devlin would show Jessica what kind of a monster he was before it was too late.

chapter ten

'Tracy!' Jessica pounded the door as the cloudy afternoon sky threatened rain. 'I know you're in there!'

The door to her sister's condominium remained firmly locked. She noticed the neighbour's curtains twitching from across the walkway. How ridiculous she must look yelling at an inanimate object.

Jessica wondered if Tracy was really away. Nah. Her car was parked in its designated spot. Obviously she was waiting for Jessica to get embarrassed by this public scene.

Well, two can play at this game, Jessica decided. She may not be the grand master of mind games, but she had already picked up a few pointers in the last few days.

'Tracy Parks,' Jessica called out loudly, feeling the pull on her vocal chords. 'I will pound on this door until it drives you crazy. I don't care if I'm making a scene. You open up, right now!'

She was surprised to hear the scratch of the metal locks. 'God, Jessica.' The door swung open. 'What are you trying to do? Get me evicted?'

'Hello, Tracy,' she responded cheerfully. 'What are you trying to do? Evict me from your life?'

Tracy rolled her eyes. 'You are so melodramatic. Come on in,' she added ungraciously. 'No need to display our dirty laundry to all of Seattle.'

'An exaggeration, don't you think?' Jessica asked, as she stepped into her sister's contemporary monochromatic condo. Everything was white, from the carpeting to the furniture, to the accessories. Jessica shivered, always aware of the brittle coldness of the décor.

'Oooh,' Tracy taunted as she slammed the door shut. 'You've learned how to backtalk since becoming a wife.'

Jessica faced her twin. 'What do you mean?' She didn't feel the need to back down or apologise. It felt liberating.

'You're much more...vocal. Sex does that to you? Tell me.' Tracy's narrowed eyes couldn't hide the stark pain. 'Are you this vocal with Devlin? I didn't take you for a screamer, more like a crier.'

Jessica blushed from the straight talk. 'I didn't realize that you were obsessed with my sex life,' she replied witheringly. 'Maybe you should get one of your own.'

Tracy's eyes widened with admiration. 'Good one.' She folded her arms defensively across her chest. 'I'm just wondering how good it must be that you would choose your husband of one day over your own twin sister.'

Jessica's shoulders sagged. 'It's not like that.' She reached out and placed her hand on Tracy's arm. 'I'm not choosing.'

'Oh, I see.' She brushed Jessica off. 'You're greedy. You want both.'

'Why not?' As far as Jessica was concerned, she needed the people who cared about her in her life. Her mother and sister may not be able to help, may not be strong enough to protect her, but at least she didn't have to go through life alone.

'Don't you get it?' Tracy stared at her sister with disbelief. 'Devlin is the enemy,' she stated with exaggerated slowness. 'You are sleeping with the enemy.'

Anger mushroomed inside Jessica. She tried her best to push it down. 'I am trying to make the best of an impossible situation. Look, I didn't come here to argue.'

'Really?' Tracy walked to the living area. 'Could have

fooled me the way you were pounding on my door.'

Jessica ignored the bid to start another argument and followed her sister. 'I'm here to invite you to a dinner party.'

'At your house?' Tracy was incredulous. 'Are you insane?' She sat on the sofa with her sister. 'Does Devlin know you're here?'

Jessica paused. He didn't know and she vividly recalled the last tug-of-war. 'He knows I want to invite you,' she replied carefully.

Tracy checked her manicure. 'What did he say to that?'

She decided to give the censored version. There was no need to stir up bad blood. 'He said it was a waste of time because you would throw the invitation back in my face.'

Tracy's nostrils flared. 'He's right.' She didn't look too happy over the fact.

'Please, Tracy,' Jessica begged. 'Please say you'll come. I need you there.'

She hesitated before shaking her head in refusal. 'You don't need me anymore.' Tracy's ragged voice pulled at Jessica's heartstrings.

'Are you kidding?' She leaned forward, her voice thick with desperation. 'I need you more than ever. Especially at the party. Barry is going to be there,' she confided.

'Not my problem,' Tracy shrugged, the casual move belying the challenge glittering in her eyes. 'You're the idiot who invited him.'

'My mother-in-law will be there,' Jessica added in an unenthusiastic voice.

'You're the one who got married.'

And you're the one who got me into the situation. Jessica reined in the thought before she said it aloud. 'And you're my sister,' she reminded. 'I love you and…'

Tracy cast a jealous look. 'Love me more than Devlin?'

Jessica bolted from the sofa. 'This is not a competition!'

She moved for the door. 'Just forget it.'

'Wait a second.' Tracy studied her sister. 'You didn't answer me. Do you love Devlin?'

She turned sharply to her sister. She was unable to hide what she concealed every minute of the day. Her eyes were shadowed by a cynical mist, snuffing out the last glimmer of romantic hope. Her cheeks, vibrant from the first flush of passion were paling from her constant vulnerability. Her mouth tightened with the agony of unrequited love.

'Hell!' Tracy tossed up her hands. 'You're in love with him! Don't you know any better?'

'I-I...' she wanted to deny it. She couldn't be in love with a man who could destroy her without remorse. But she was. She had known it for a long time, but had tried to ignore the truth. Now she was face-to-face with it and still couldn't cope. Jessica stumbled to the sofa and collapsed. 'What am I going to do?'

Tracy's answer was swift and absolute. 'There's only one thing to do. Forget what he has on you – to blazes with it. You have to leave him.'

Jessica shook her head vigorously. 'I can't do that.'

'Leave him while you still have the power to leave. Stop shaking your head at me. Why not leave? He'd do it to you in a heartbeat. He doesn't need you. He certainly doesn't love you.'

Tears smarted her eyes. 'I know.' But she couldn't banish the image of Devlin alone. Deserted and abandoned. Considering his strength and power, the image was senseless. Yet Jessica knew she couldn't walk away from him.

'You can't change him,' Tracy said. 'No one can make Devlin Hunter fall in love. He doesn't understand the emotion.'

The tears began to sting in earnest. 'I know that too.'

'He's going to break your heart. Stomp it into pieces and throw it away.'

'Stop trying to comfort me,' she hissed, as the first scalding tear hit her lashes.

'I'm not trying to. I'm just stating the facts.' Tracy sighed and curved her arm around Jessica's defeated figure. 'But I'll be here to pick up the pieces.'

'Thanks,' Jessica sniffed. She wiped the streaming tears from her cheeks.

'I'll try to make it to the dinner, OK?' Tracy said grudgingly. 'After all, what are sisters for?'

Jessica twisted her hands nervously as she studied the table setting. She had used the finest tablecloth and fresh-cut flower centrepieces. The silverware, crystal and china, gleaming under the modern chandelier, were of the highest quality. Rodgers and Jessica had decided on a menu that was deceptively simple, showcasing the freshest produce and the cook's flair.

It probably wasn't good enough for her guests. Carlotta would find fault, and her mother would sprinkle the dinner conversation with a few helpful 'suggestions'. Barry would sneer at his plate, make a show of refusing it, and then fill his stomach with a steady stream of alcohol.

Strangely, it didn't matter. Jessica saw the table through her eyes and not those of her relatives. Every decision she had made for the meal reflected the values of her home and family. Pride welled in her chest at the display she set with her husband in mind. The finished result was alive and vibrant. Maybe if she and Devlin focused on their relationship with the same attention, they might have a chance.

She heard Devlin's soft, steady footfall. She turned around and caught her breath as he appeared at the doorway.

His dark suit emphasized the strong, lean body she now knew so well. She wished for the umpteenth time that she had the nerve to cancel dinner. She'd rather spend her evening curled up with Devlin.

Devlin's mouth twisted in a knowing smile. Jessica blushed and hurried to speak to cover up her response. 'You look very nice, Devlin,' she said, deciding her lame words were an understatement.

'You're beautiful.' The words were torn out of his throat. The raw tone and dusky eyes were at odds with his sophistication.

Jessica ducked her head. 'Thank you.' The sapphire silk dress was a recent purchase and the superb cut leant elegance to her new image of corporate wife. The rich colour was also the perfect backdrop for her wedding ring. From the possessive gleam in Devlin's eye, her choice did not go unnoticed. She nervously wetted her lips with her tongue. 'Do you think the table looks all right?'

'Yes,' he answered brusquely.

'Are you sure?' she insisted, sensing he hadn't glanced at the furniture. She felt his gaze warming her. 'I've never given a dinner party before.'

He sighed. 'Your family will remember the party,' he replied quietly. 'Not the details.'

She frowned. 'That's true.' At first she thought Devlin was distracted, but she was wrong. Regret coloured his words.

'Jess.' He stepped forward and urgency threaded his voice. His eyes demanded for attention, for understanding.

She backed away with uncertainty. 'Yes?'

He paused, trying to find a way to form the words. Jessica's heart skipped. 'Everything I do,' he began, 'everything I've done is to protect you.'

Jessica blinked, confused. Protect? Against what? 'I don't

need protection,' she assured him, 'but I appreciate your concern.'

'Jess.' He clasped his fingers around her wrist. 'Listen to me.'

'Good evening,' Carlotta Hunter announced gaily as she entered the room. 'My dear, what a lovely table. You've outdone yourself.'

Jessica escaped from her husband's hold. 'Thank you, Mrs Hunter.' She peered around Devlin to see that her mother-in-law was wearing an exuberant red silk pantsuit. The woman's demeanour pulsated with energy. 'I hope you enjoy the dinner.'

'Oh, I'm sure I will.' Her eyes nearly bulged with anticipation. 'I've been looking forward to it.'

'Mother,' Devlin growled. He vibrated with a barely-leashed menace. Jessica quashed the instinct to hold him back.

'Don't worry about me, Devlin.' Her mouth twisted into an odd smile. 'I will be the life of the party.'

'Or the death of it,' he muttered under his breath. Jessica gave him a warning jab with her elbow as the doorbell rang. Devlin entwined her arms at the crook of his elbow. The protective gesture worried Jessica. What did he want to protect her from?

'Wonderful! The guests have arrived.' Carlotta whirled around and exited the dining room with a flourish.

They followed the older woman to the entrance. 'Your mother really seems to live for a party,' Jessica said out of the corner of her mouth.

'More like for *this* party.' His alert gaze scanned the room. Devlin's muscles bunched under his dark suit. He was ready to attack at the slightest provocation.

Jessica knew she had better keep an eye on him. She didn't have time to figure out the problem as Rodgers opened the door, allowing Barry and Lorraine Parks inside. Jessica hurried to greet them.

'Mom.' She accepted quick pecks on both cheeks from her mother. 'I'm glad you could make it.' Jessica reluctantly turned to her stepfather, whose eyes were riveted on Carlotta.

'Mrs Hunter,' Jessica hurried with the introduction, 'I'd like you to meet my stepfather, Barry Parks. Barry, this is Devlin's mother, Carlotta Hunter.'

Barry froze in mid-step. The pose appeared outrageous for the dynamic businessman who bulldozed his way through life. 'Carlotta?' he repeated, like a man trapped between the present and his memories.

'Hello, Barry, it's been a long time.' Carlotta slid up to him and greeted him with a breezy kiss on the cheek. 'How have you been?'

'You two know each other?' Jessica asked, absently ushering them to the sitting room. She grimaced at her inane observation but Barry didn't strike back with a snide put-down. She wondered how much Carlotta's presence had unsettled her stepfather.

'Oh, I used to be from around here,' Carlotta revealed, her eyes glowing like shards of green glass. 'I'm not a native Australian.'

'Is that right?' Jessica wasn't sure what to say. 'Oh, and this is my mother, Lorraine Parks. Mom, Carlotta Hunter.'

Lorraine politely offered her hand to the woman. Carlotta briefly glanced at it, and then shot a venomous look at Lorraine before turning her back. She strode into the living room, ignoring Devlin's warning glare.

Jessica's eyes were still wide from the blatant rebuke. 'I'm sorry about my mother-in-law,' Jessica whispered her apology as she escorted her mother to the sofa. She patted Lorraine's arm, attempting to comfort her mother's jangled sensibilities. Lorraine wouldn't stand up to Carlotta's in-your-face brand of contempt. It wasn't a matter of etiquette or being a lady. Her mother was too fragile, too scared of the counterattack.

'Don't be,' her mother softly replied. 'You're not responsible for that dreadful woman.' She tried for a wry smile, but her wavering lips and wounded eyes ruined the effect.

Jessica smiled wearily. 'It's going to be a long night.' She wanted to escape and hide in her room more than ever.

'Welcome to the world of an executive wife. I have a bad feeling about this. No one surprises Barry.'

Jessica mutely nodded. She offered her mother a seat next to her stepfather. Her mother-in-law was already sitting on the chair adjacent to the sofa, as if she were a queen sitting on her throne.

Rodgers had already set out a fruit-and-cheese tray that would accompany the chilled Chardonnay. Jessica had been ravenous for the juicy pears and aromatic cheese, but her appetite was now missing in action.

She searched for Devlin. He seemed unusually subdued, already presenting Barry a crystal tumbler of amber liquid. As if he had it prepared because he knew Barry would need it. Jessica tossed the thought aside as Devlin returned to the bar, noticing that her husband showed no interest in joining the group. He stood back like an observer, or maybe more like a guard.

'OK, Carlotta.' Barry had decided he had had enough of the good manners. 'Let's cut the bull.' He leaned forward and rested his elbows on his knees. 'What brings you here?'

'My son, of course.' She hid a secretive smile behind her wineglass.

'Uh-uh.' Barry shook his head. 'Your son got married a few days ago but you didn't see fit to come to the wedding.

Now, all of a sudden, you're here? Doesn't jive.'

'Barry!' Jessica knew all the answers lurked under the tension. She preferred them to stay put, at least until dessert when she could reasonably throw her relatives out of her house.

Barry flashed Jessica a silencing glance. His brown eyes appeared darker, more dangerous, against his ashen complexion. Jessica was far from relieved to see the human expression flitting across her stepfather's face. She knew he was not in control. Normally, that would make her stand up and cheer.

'Oh, Barry.' Carlotta gave a lilting laugh, but it struck a sour note. 'You know me so well. I guess you should, considering our past.'

Terrific. Jessica's shoulders wilted. Barry and Carlotta were once lovers. *Just terrific.* She glanced at the door. Where was Tracy? Her twin could provide some sort of distraction. Jessica would embrace any interruption, even a food fight!

'That was a long time ago.' Barry gave his ex-lover an once-over. 'You've changed.'

Carlotta shrugged delicately. 'But the past doesn't. Like the way you jilted me at the altar.'

Jessica cringed at the bitter hurt in her mother-in-law's voice. Carlotta and Barry were once engaged? This did not bode well.

'Are you still harping over that?' He pulled out a handkerchief and wiped the sweat surfacing on his forehead. 'All right, all right. I could have approached it differently. There. Does that make you happy?'

'Not really,' Carlotta responded dryly. 'I wonder if you regret having pirated my family's business. Do you think you handled destroying my family in a wrong manner? Are you sorry that you ruined my life?'

Jessica hurried to where Devlin stood. 'Devlin', she whispered. 'We have to stop this.' She had a feeling anything she said to interrupt would feed the antagonism, giving it the power to grow into open hate. Devlin knew his mother best. He would think of something.

Devlin looked down at his drink. 'No.'

Time stood still. Jessica felt like she was treading through a void. Once she broke the surface, everything would move again. 'No?'

'It needs to happen so life can move on.' His face held no emotion and his voice originated from a secretive chamber in his tarnished heart.

She felt her face blench. 'You mean you knew about this?' she accused.

The muscle in his jaw spasmed. 'Yes.'

'That's it? That's all you have to say to me?' Why didn't he warn her? Unless he saw her as the enemy.

Barry's loud voice intruded the fiercely whispered exchange. 'Your family got what it deserved. Your father didn't think anything about destroying my family or leaving us penniless. I was determined to destroy you the same way.'

Jessica watched, horrified, as Barry leaned back into the sofa, his satisfied smile growing. He absently rubbed his right arm. Jessica's brow knitted with concern.

'Your determination paid off,' Carlotta conceded. 'You deserted your bride at the altar, just as my uncle did to your mother. You invaded the executive echelon of the business and stole all of our clients and our future. The collapse of our family soon followed, just as yours did.'

'I don't know why you're taking this personally.' Barry took a sip of his liquor and smacked his lips. Jessica watched with revulsion as the older man gloried in his past schemes, as if his sordid past actions were on display for a tribute.

Carlotta's face sharpened with cold fury. 'My name was ruined because of you. I moved across the world to escape the mess you caused.'

'Sorry, Carlotta. You just got in the way. I would try to explain it to you, but women just can't wrap their brains around the concept of "an eye for an eye".'

Carlotta suddenly leaned back in her chair, recapturing her queen of the world demeanour. 'I understand that philosophy very well. So does my son, Devlin.'

'I'm sure he does,' Barry said in a patronising manner. He rolled his eyes for the benefit of the unwilling spectators.

'Hmm.' She struck a thoughtful pose, tapping a blood-red nail against her chin. 'And it seems that he's invaded the executive echelon of your company.'

Barry waved away the possibility of a threat. 'He's young and untried. I can oust him out before the week is through. And, in case you didn't notice, he didn't continue the revenge cycle. He didn't jilt my stepdaughter at the altar.'

'He didn't follow the revenge exactly,' Carlotta spared a vicious glance at her son, who appeared disinterested with the trip down memory lane. 'But I'm sure he has his reasons.'

'He doesn't have the stomach for revenge. It doesn't burn in him like it does in us. He's no threat to me, but he can try. Bring it on, Devlin,' Barry incited, puffing with confidence. Devlin met the elder man's gaze but gave no response.

'We are a threat,' Carlotta stated with supreme confidence. 'For all you know, Devlin could have stolen your clients. Your future.'

'I'm not worried.' Barry kicked back the fiery liquor in a showy display of machismo. 'I'll destroy him – and you – before he can figure out what to do with them.'

'And once you lose what money you have left, your "family dynasty",' she sneered at the word, 'will collapse.'

The prediction was meaningless. 'They aren't my family. I have no heir.'

'Oh.' Carlotta's eyes sparkled maliciously. 'But that is where you are wrong.'

'My stepdaughters may have my name, but they don't get my legacy. Sorry, Carlotta. You didn't get to complete the cycle. If I had a natural heir,' he tossed a severe look of censure at Lorraine, 'he could claim my fortune, but that ain't going to happen.'

'No, you misunderstand. You do have an heir.' Her smile was pure evil.

Barry's forehead pleated with a frown. 'What are you talking about?'

'Haven't you figured it out?' Carlotta mocked. She toyed with the terse silence in the room like a seasoned actress. 'When you fulfilled your revenge by deserting me at the altar, I was already pregnant.'

Barry's mouth sagged open. The crystal tumbler dropped from his fingers and it hit the wooden floor with a thud. Lorraine lunged for the cup, her need to focus on an inanimate object painfully apparent.

'Looking at you once again,' Carlotta continued the chatty tone, as if she didn't drop a life-altering titbit of information. 'I see quite a resemblance.'

Barry heaved in a gasp of air. And another. His loose fist jerked to his chest.

'Barry?' Lorraine asked fearfully, placing a concerned hand on his arm. He didn't brush her away. The lack of Barry's disdain alarmed Jessica.

'And not just physically,' Carlotta continued in a drawl, 'but the same ruthlessness.'

Panic gripped Jessica. 'Something's wrong.' Her voice rose octaves with each syllable.

'He's having a heart attack.' Devlin threw down his glass.

He ignored the sprinkling crash of crystal as he rushed to Barry. 'Call an ambulance.'

Carlotta leaned forward, determined to receive all of Barry's attention. 'The same, what did you call it, Jessica? The same code of honour.'

Barry's glazed eyes squinted. 'You mean…?'

'Yes, Barry. Devlin is your son.'

chapter eleven

Doors crashing. Medical staff running down corridors. The overwhelming scent of disinfectant. Crisis pulsing through the atmosphere. Flashing lights and beeping alarms puncturing through Jessica's foggy mind.

'I can't believe this is happening,' Lorraine said again. Jessica placed her hand on top of her mother's and gave a reassuring squeeze.

They sat in a private waiting room inside the Cardiology ward. The colours and décor were intended to calm family and friends. As far as Jessica was concerned, it wasn't working. She was battling the rising wave of hysteria.

'Everything will be fine, Mom,' she said. Again. 'Barry will pull through. You know him. He refuses to admit defeat.'

A ghost of a smile flickered on Lorraine's trembling mouth. 'That's true.' Her face grew serious, obviously remembering Barry's determined expression not to succumb to the attack. Jessica would have gladly kicked herself for accidentally conjuring the memory.

'What if he…dies?' Lorraine's voice wavered. 'What is going to become of me? Jessica, I am forty-five years old. I don't have any skills and I have no money. What am I going to do?'

Jessica didn't judge the self-centred outburst. She understood her mother's fears. Lorraine may despise Barry, but he had always provided for her financially. Jessica wondered if the heart attack was a wake-up call for the older woman. Would her mother realize her tenuous situation as a penniless widow? Would she do anything about her circumstances or look toward her daughters for help?

Jessica decided she would take care of her mother, no matter what her own living situation would be. The decision was scary and cathartic at the same time. She realized at some time, that she had ceased to be the person that needed to be babysat. She had suddenly become the one who could give and take care of another.

'Mom, I will take care of you. You won't be destitute. I'll make sure of it, OK?' She gave another sympathetic pat to her mother's hand and glanced at the clock. The timepiece must be broken. It had registered only a few moments but it felt like an eternity had passed.

'I wonder what's taking Tracy so long. I'm going to go walk around the entrance.' She felt torn. Jessica knew she should stay with her mother, but if she didn't walk around she would split in two.

Her mother nodded and began to chew on a manicured nail. 'I'll be all right.' She watched the door, patiently waiting to see the attending physician.

'I'll bring you something to eat,' Jessica promised, deciding that the food should be very sugary to zap her mother's shock. She quietly left the room and exited the ward. The hallways were now brightly lit but the stench of cleaners still permeated the air.

Turning toward the main entrance of the building, Jessica faltered to a stop. Devlin stood against the wall, his tie and jacket discarded. He raked a hand through his hair. From the untidiness of his hair, it appeared he'd been doing that for a while.

Jessica wasn't ready to see him. Not after that little bombshell his mother had dropped. She pivoted on her heel, intending to go in the opposite direction. The move caught Devlin's attention.

'Any news?' Devlin asked.

Jessica remained where she was with her back to her husband. 'No. Not yet.' She still couldn't believe it. The man she loved was Barry's son! Jessica controlled the shiver coursing down her spine.

'Is your mother all right by herself?' His voice sounded closer, but she didn't hear him move. *Only a fool would turn their back on Devlin Hunter.* The same could be said about Barry Parks.

She whirled around. 'Why don't you go in and check for yourself?' she asked angrily. Why should he care? He had stood by as Carlotta had torn a man down. He didn't lift a finger when Jessica asked him to stop it from happening.

Devlin looked at the door to the Cardiology wing. 'I thought it would be best if I stayed out here.'

'Why?' she asked, not caring if she sounded aggressive. She wanted to wring his neck. She wanted to tear him into little pieces. Instead she said, 'the waiting room is for family. You're more family than any of us.' She flicked one last glance at him and turned away.

'Jess…' Anguish seeped in his voice. He reached out, but then let his arm fall back.

She couldn't bear to look at him. 'Why didn't you tell me?' Her voice broke as she mentioned the cutting betrayal.

'My parentage doesn't matter between you and me,' he rasped. 'Don't you remember saying that to my mother?'

He was twisting her words, twisting the situation to his advantage. Just like Barry. 'It mattered enough for you to complete the revenge. It mattered enough to marry me. In fact,' she raised her swollen, red eyes and watched the stony expression on his face. 'Why did you marry me? The clause was to be a Parks or marry one. All you needed to do was prove your heritage.'

'If I was to follow the revenge exactly, I needed to abandon you at the altar. Barry would get the social embarrassment he deserved. Had it been Tracy at the altar, she would have taken the jilting on the chin. In fact, she would use the event to prove that she was willing to sacrifice everything for the company. You, on the other hand, would have suffered. I felt it necessary to protect you.'

Jessica gave a short bark of cynical laughter. 'By getting me deeper into the situation?' She didn't need his form of protection. She needed protection *from* him.

'By getting you out of Seattle when Barry found out about the switch,' Devlin argued. 'I wanted you out of his house when he found out the real reason why I was so interested in his company.'

'Well, thanks for your concern. It's something I could have done without.' She lowered her voice as an orderly walked by and glared at her. She glared right back before returning her attention to Devlin. 'It might be a while before we hear something from the doctors.' She paused. 'Where is your mother?'

'At home.' Devlin's face tightened. The skin stretched across his face. He looked older. Harsher. 'I've arranged for her to leave the country immediately.'

She shook her head at the carnage the woman had made. 'Why couldn't you have done it sooner?' Why couldn't he have left everything alone? He didn't need the money or prestige. But, it was all a game for him. She was just a game piece to collect.

'The revenge had been brewing since well before I was born.' He turned his head away from her. 'I was raised to complete it. I needed it to play out so I could move on with my life.'

'Move on with Parks Systems. Congratulations,' she said bitterly. 'Excuse me if I don't jump for joy.'

'I don't want it.' Devlin's eyes flashed angrily. 'I never did.'

'I'm not stupid,' she bit out. 'Of course you want it. You trained over thirty years for this moment. So what if you might have a death on your hands because of it?'

'The moment Barry is out of danger, I'm resigning as CEO.'

What game was he playing at now? 'Sure you are.'

'I've never lied to you, Jess. Why should I start now?'

'You're right,' she said waspishly. 'Why start lying when omitting pertinent facts and concealing the truth has worked so well for you in the past.' She wondered about what he said. If he had told her the truth, what aspect was he hiding? A horrifying thought occurred to her. 'You're resigning so that you can make your mother CEO.'

'I would never do that. Parks is your family's livelihood and I am responsible for it. If you must know, I've been grooming Nicholas to take my place.'

'Aha.' Now she understood his angle. 'You don't want Parks, but you are doing everything in your power to keep control. By putting one of your men in charge.' She moved forward until she was toe-to-toe with him. 'If you wanted to right a wrong, you would put Tracy in charge.'

Devlin reluctantly shook his head. 'Tracy is not loyal to the company. Do you know what she was doing while you were masquerading as a bride? She was trying to secretly purchase more company stock. She was planning a takeover.'

'No, she wasn't.' Takeover? Was Devlin insane? Tracy was a member of the family who owned the business. There was no need to oust Barry. Obviously Devlin was trying to take advantage of her business ignorance. 'She was trying to hire a programmer.'

'I might as well tell you, since no one else found it

necessary to clue you in.' He exhaled sharply. 'There was no programmer. I wouldn't fire an executive over something as trivial as that.'

Jessica automatically shook her head. 'I don't believe you.' He was trying to play with her mind and make her doubt her sister. Divide and conquer the Parks family.

'Yeah, why should you?' Devlin sighed. 'Obviously this is not the time to discuss it. Go home and I'll call you if there's any news.'

She bristled at his command. 'I'm not going anywhere.' She wasn't going to listen to him ever again.

'You're dead on your feet.' His eyes took in her pale complexion and dark shadows under her puffy eyes.

'And I'm certainly not stepping foot into your house. I'd rather live in a cardboard box, in the street.'

'I get the picture.' Devlin's jaw tightened with anger. 'But as my wife...'

'Your soon to be ex-wife,' she corrected. 'It was bad enough that you blackmail me into marriage, carrying around the embarrassment that "any sister will do". But I can't stomach the fact that I'm embroiled in your revenge plan.'

'You're conveniently forgetting that your family tricked you into a plan bent on destroying Barry.'

'Stop it! Stop making such vile accusations!' Jessica tried to tame the wildness tearing at her from inside. Her throat ached as she tapped down the need to shriek. 'My family is not like yours. We could never be so...so malicious.'

'I'm malicious for seeking justice?' Devlin shook his head. 'How can you say that? You don't even like Barry,' he said starkly.

'You're right. I don't like him. He needs to destroy everything around him. I escaped his home as quickly as I could. And do you know what? You're very similar to him.'

Devlin paled. His shoulders stooped forward, like he'd

been confronted by his darkest fear. 'I am not like Barry at all,' he whispered.

'You tried to destroy him and everything he touched. And soon you'll try to destroy me. Oh, but you don't even have to try. I'll just get in the way.'

Devlin grabbed her wrist. 'My family's revenge was nothing like Barry's. If you would just take a moment to understand.'

She ripped her wrist away from his touch. 'I'm beginning to understand. Maybe I'm wrong, Devlin. I'm understanding what hate and the need to avenge feels like. It might be a part of your DNA, but maybe Barry bred it into me as well. Right now, it's burning inside me. Is that how it feels to you too? Who knows, maybe I can continue the cycle for you.'

'Stop talking rubbish,' he growled. Devlin looked like he was caught in a never-ending nightmare. Jessica refused to indulge in the luxury of caring, reminding herself that it was a nightmare of his own making. A nightmare he had dragged her into.

'Rubbish?' she challenged. 'Why would you think that? You think I don't have the power? Maybe I do. For all you know, I could be pregnant with the son who will have the power to destroy you.'

Devlin flinched. 'Jess, are you saying…?'

'I'm not saying anything,' she snarled. 'Especially not to you. You've poisoned everything around you, and I'm not going to let it happen to me. Stay away from me and my family.'

Jessica stormed off, refusing to look back. She was relieved and surprised that she was successful with her escape. Devlin didn't try to stop her.

Several days later, Jessica and Tracy left Barry's hospital

room. Barry was beginning to be his old vicious self. The brush with death didn't make him into a crabby teddy bear. It made him more determined than ever to conquer the world in what time he had left.

Jessica breathed with relief as her duty visit ended. She pulled her twin aside in the disinfectant-smelling hallway. 'Tracy, I need to ask you a big favour.' She could barely form the words. She was incredibly tired from lack of sleep and lack of appetite. Jessica couldn't focus on anything other than the misery of life without Devlin.

'What kind of favour?' Tracy asked with her trademark scepticism.

Jessica chewed her inner lip. 'I need you to pretend to be me. Just for fifteen minutes.'

Tracy's shoes squeaked as she skidded to a stop. 'Are you crazy? Do you see where that got us the last time?'

'I know, I know,' Jessica said apologetically. 'But I need to get some stuff from Devlin's home.' She had made the tactical error of declaring that she would not step foot in Devlin's house, forgetting that all her sentimental treasures were there.

'Tell your butler to gather it and leave it by the door,' Tracy suggested. 'We'll do a drive-by and grab it.'

Jessica shook her head. She had already tried that. 'Rodgers was given strictest orders not to assist me.'

'Really?' Tracy frowned as she mulled over the piece of information. 'That's strange. I wonder why.'

She shrugged. 'Devlin doesn't think my leaving home will resolve any problems.' Why did he have to drag out their separation? Was there another element of the revenge she should know about?

'He doesn't want you to leave?' Tracy's eyebrows rose sky-high. 'Let me see if I have got this straight. He wants to stay married to you?'

Jessica frowned ferociously. 'What are you looking at?' She knew that look. 'Get your mind out of the gutter. Sex has nothing to do with it.' At least, she thought it didn't. 'I think he wants to stay married to me while he's acting head of Parks. It makes for a smoother transition.'

'I don't know about that.' Tracy twisted her mouth thoughtfully. 'I thought you and Devlin had an arranged marriage kind of deal.'

'We do – or did, rather.' Jessica started to get flustered. 'We didn't have a marriage like Mom and Barry.'

'Stranger and stranger.' Tracy acted like she saw more than what was explained. Jessica wasn't sure if that was a good thing.

'Exactly.' Jessica gave a decisive nod. Now was not the time to listen to Tracy's hypotheses about her relationship. 'Devlin's proving to be difficult. All I want to do is get some of my stuff out of the house.'

'I don't know, Jessie. If you start sneaking around, he's going to be even more difficult. He can drag a divorce out for years.'

'All the more reason to get what is mine and get out of there.' She didn't want to deal with Devlin. She needed to get away so she could mend and grow strong without him. 'I don't want find my stuff "damaged" when I finally get it.' Jessica felt a streak of disloyalty. She knew Devlin wasn't like that, but she wanted Tracy's help.

'You have a point.' Tracy sighed. 'And I was just getting used to Devlin.'

'What?' Jessica's mouth fell open. 'Are you crazy? You hate him, remember? He's the *enemy*. Any of this ring a bell?'

'Yeah, I know, but he's turning out to be a very decent brother-in-law. You should have seen the severance pay he sent me.' She gave an appreciative whistle.

'He didn't send it to you,' Jessica felt obliged to point out. 'Parks Software Systems was legally obligated.'

'Nope. The cheque was extremely generous. I thought it was an error and called my friend in Payroll. It appears that Devlin wanted to make amends.'

It was a trick. It had nothing to do with what he said about their livelihood. He said it so she would *think* he was doing it all for them. Jessica rubbed her forehead. Devlin's mind was so confusing. 'If he wanted to make amends, he would have given you your job back.'

Tracy considered the idea. Her blue eyes lacked the glow of competition. 'If he offered it, I wouldn't take it.'

Jessica froze in shock. 'Are you serious?' Tracy didn't want to pursue her childhood goal of working for the family business?

'Yeah. I want to create a business of my own. Probably something in computers. Hey...' Her eyes brightened. 'Maybe the two of us could become partners.'

When pigs fly. 'Scary thought,' Jessica responded. 'But you wanted to work for Parks.'

'I wanted to *control* Parks,' she clarified. 'Big difference.'

Jessica's stomach churned over her sister's true motives. 'Tracy, there was no computer programmer, was there?' she asked hesitantly. She had a bad feeling that she wouldn't like the answer.

Tracy looked suitably chagrined. 'You figured that out, huh? No, I was trying to buy some stock from some discouraged stockholders. Only Devlin found out about it and got to them before I could.'

'Why didn't you tell me?' She couldn't stop voicing the hurt that ballooned inside her. Devlin had told her the truth and she had dismissed it out of hand. But did he tell her out of his sense of protection? Or out of his need to destroy the Parks family?

Tracy wrapped her arm around Jessica's shoulder and gave it a sisterly squeeze. 'You wouldn't have gone through the rehearsal dinner. You would have told me to forget about that crazy scheme.'

'You're right. I would have.' Jessica noticed her sister's lack of apology. Wasn't she aware that the trust between them would suffer from this point on? Jessica knew, without a doubt, that it would be a long, long time before she'd do another favour for Tracy.

'And you need to forget this crazy scheme of yours.' She patted Jessica's arm. 'It's not going to work. Too much could go wrong. I think we found that out the hard way.'

'I know, but I want my stuff. I've tried everything else, but Devlin keeps messing with my plans so I have to go back.' She shook her head. 'I can't go back into that house, Tracy. I just can't.'

'Bad memories, huh?' Tracy clucked her tongue knowingly.

'Worse.' Fragmented images flickered through her mind. Devlin's protective arm around her shoulders. A shared smile. A sense of cherishment and belonging. Jessica closed her eyes and blocked the images. It was all a lie. It was a means to an end. 'Good memories.'

Tracy pondered the situation. 'I'm only going to say this once, and I can't believe I'm saying this at all.' She wrinkled her face and spat the words out. 'You should go back to him.'

'No.' It was impossible. Not only did she say unforgivable things to him, but also nothing had changed between them. 'I don't want to wind up like Mom.'

'Amen to that,' Tracy said with depth of feeling. 'But I don't think that will happen any time soon. You've developed a very big mouth lately.'

Jessica gave her sister a playful shove. 'So are you going to help me out or not?' she asked hopefully.

'Sure.' Tracy smiled. 'I never got to play the good twin before.'

Jessica crouched down in the passenger seat of her car. Even though she was facing away from Devlin's home, she didn't want to be spotted by Rodgers. Why Tracy felt it necessary for her to be around escaped logic. A former executive should be able to follow a short list of items without her sister. Jessica was feeling a little bit smug at the thought. *She* faced an entire congregation as the wrong bride without her twin nearby.

The cloak-and-dagger mood probably was ridiculous, Jessica conceded as she watched the reflection of the rear view mirror. It was a workday and Devlin would be at Parks lording over his spoiled goods. Rodgers had no power to refuse Jessica into the house. He may have been given orders to prevent Jessica's entrance, but no authority.

Rodgers appeared at the door and greeted Tracy with a warm smile. He quickly ushered her inside. He seemed to accept Tracy as Jessica. There wasn't any reason not to. Dressed in baggy jeans and a T-shirt, Tracy completed the image by plaiting her hair into a loose braid.

She hoped Tracy didn't dawdle. The list of possessions she needed to take was brief but essential. After she loaded up her stuff, there would be no tangible link between Devlin and her, other than her wedding ring.

Jessica glanced down at the sapphire gem. She should return it. Devlin might have had a brief moment of kindness by giving her a ring of her own, but the reasons behind it were the same. It was a prop for the sake of appearances.

Sighing, Jessica returned her attention to the mirror. She gasped, her eyes widening and her heart racing, as she saw Devlin striding towards her. Her mind spluttered with questions – How? Why? Where could she hide?

Jessica leaped into action. She immediately locked the doors before realizing that the windows were opened. She pushed the button, but the window didn't budge because the keys weren't in the car.

'Oh, no,' she sobbed. She frantically pulled at the lock, determined to make a run for it. Devlin got there before she could open the door.

He wrenched the door away from her hand. He loomed over her like a sinister shadow. 'Jess, get out of the damn car.'

'No.' One moment she wanted in, then out, now in again. Her head spun from it all. Why did she listen to her sister? When would she ever learn?

Devlin didn't give her another chance. He delved inside and grabbed her around the waist, hauling her out on to the brick driveway. His arms were bands of steel, wrapping her close to him.

'Let go of me this instant!' she shrieked. 'Do you hear me? Devlin Hunter, I'm warning you!'

Devlin appeared deaf to her commands. He slammed the door shut and the force rattled the car. He firmly gathered her and then half-dragged, half-carried her across the driveway.

'What have you done to my sister?' she yelled as she dug her heels into the gravel. 'If you so much as touch her, if there is one hair out of place on her head...'

'She's in the house,' Devlin cut through her ranting. 'Unharmed.'

'Not by her own choice, I'm sure,' Jessica spat out, kicking her legs to slow him down.

'That is your opinion,' Devlin said coolly as he lugged her to the house. 'Perhaps she realized that we needed to talk.'

Talk? No way. He would double-talk her into confusion

until she promised him everything. 'We can do that through our lawyers.'

'That will be a waste of time since we are right here.'

'I don't want to talk to you,' she replied mulishly. She just wanted out. Out of the situation and out of town.

'Fine.' Strained patience weighed down his voice. 'I will do the talking.'

Jessica concentrated on trying to get out of his grasp. It proved impossible.

He suddenly stopped. She almost fell on her bottom from the quick halt. Grasping her from under his arms, he positioned her so that she had to look in his face.

She could feel his searching gaze. It lasted so long that she wondered if he was memorising her every feature.

'I miss you,' he said rawly.

Her heart clenched. 'No, you don't. You might miss me in bed, but...'

'I miss *you*,' he emphasized, 'and I want you back. As my wife.'

Her traitorous heart sang at his words. She swallowed awkwardly. 'I'm not coming back.'

'I understand how you feel and I'm determined to change your mind. Whatever it takes. I'm starting by making up for my family's actions.'

'Using caveman tactics and dragging me across your driveway is a wonderful place to start.' She glared at him. 'What's next on your list? Banging me over the head with your club?'

His brown eyes narrowed with a don't-tempt-me look. 'I have offered Tracy her old job back.'

A thousand questions crashed through her mind. She wouldn't give in and ask. It might show how much she cared! 'She doesn't want it.'

'I know. I don't blame her.' The lines bracketing Devlin's

mouth deepened. 'I've resigned as CEO. When Barry returns to the office, I'm selling all my shares and leaving the company completely.'

'Good for you.' She pressed down the urge to cheer in earnest. He had escaped from the revenge cycle. Escaped from Barry's toxic world.

Devlin's jaw tightened. 'I have your mother's evidence of her embezzlement.'

Shock jarred her body. 'What? How do you know about that?' Panic quickly overrode the shock. How was he going to use it?

'Your mother told me about it. We visited Barry several times while he was in Intensive Care. I made a deal with Barry and I have the evidence. I'm giving it to her later today.'

Why did she tell him? Why did he care? What deal did he make? What did he have to sacrifice?

No. She couldn't ask. She had to show indifference. It was her only shield, her only weapon against him. 'That has nothing to do with your family.'

'No, it doesn't. But it has something to do with us. Your Mom used that as leverage to make you walk down the aisle. She might use it again.'

'Mom isn't like that,' she hotly defended. 'It was a one-time situation.'

'Barry used it constantly,' Devlin argued. 'And I wanted the threat erased. This way you can make your own decision without any outside influences.'

She arched away from Devlin. 'What decision?'

'Divorce or marriage.' His body was tense as he handed her the power over his future. The vulnerability was foreign to him and, no matter how he tried to conceal it, his eyes dulled with fear.

Jessica frowned. The decision was hers? There had to be

a trick. 'Why don't you just use the evidence to keep me married to you?'

Devlin's fingers tightened against her back. 'Because I'm trying to prove that I'm not like Barry!' he barked out. 'I'm showing that I'm here to protect you, not contaminate your life.'

'Why do you care about my opinion?' She squinted with wariness. 'Why is that so important to you?'

'Haven't you figured it out yet? I love you.' The words sounded rusty but painfully genuine.

Jessica drew back. She desperately wanted to believe that, but she wasn't sure if she should. 'No, you don't.'

'It's true,' he said, desperation edging his voice. 'I remember our first meeting. You'd just return from college and walked into Barry's study. You were in and out of the room so fast but you managed to have enough time to knock my world sideways. I couldn't figure out why. Only when I saw you pretending to be Tracy did I understand.'

'Understand what?'

'I was drawn to your innocence. You were right. My world was poisonous. Barry tried to taint your world, but you didn't let it. You knew what you had to do to survive, but you refused to become like him.'

Jessica ducked her head with shame. 'I'm sorry I said you were like Barry. It was hateful and I only said it to hurt you.'

'I was like him,' he admitted with great reluctance. 'To a point. But I wouldn't hurt you. I don't want to destroy what you are.'

'Don't say these things.' She tried to pull away. 'I know they are not true.'

'Jess,' he pleaded, holding her tighter, drawing her closer. 'I have never lied to you. Never.'

'But you can't be in love with me.'

'I am and I'm willing to prove it. Over and over. Every

day for the rest of my life. To start with, I'm walking away from Parks and from all of my family connections.'

She wondered what had conspired between Devlin and his mother after Barry's heart attack. He obviously wasn't ready to discuss it. The regret of what could never be lurked in his brown eyes. 'What are you going to do?' she asked.

He looked away, his eyes clouded with uncertainty. 'Be a full-time husband, if you'll have me.'

'Oh,' she breathed out. That was what she wanted more than anything. She wanted it so badly she could taste it.

Devlin returned her gaze, emboldened by her telltale exclamation. 'I don't know much about family,' he admitted, 'what a real family bound by love does. Maybe you can teach me.'

'Maybe.' She slowly smiled and relaxed in his hold. 'Maybe you could teach me a few things as well.'

'And have a child,' he suggested, encouraged by her answer. 'Or two.'

Her smile grew wider. 'Possibly.' She placed her hands against his chest. His heart was beating fiercely.

'Or three,' he slipped in, the idea of expanding their home too tantalising to resist.

'You're pushing it,' she teased. A vision of brown-eyed boys running around the vineyards was alluring.

His slanted smile pierced the last icy barrier to her heart. 'No more talk about divorce?'

'No more talk,' she agreed wholeheartedly.

Devlin's expression turned serious. 'I'm not out to destroy your family. I'd rather create one with you.'

'I love you, Devlin.' She had never said that to him before, but she knew he needed to hear it. As often as possible.

Devlin's eyes glowed. Tension evaporated from his taut face. He kissed her, hard. It lacked the sophistication of his previous kisses, but it was overflowing with promise and hope.

'About damn time you said that,' he muttered against her soft lips.

She chuckled. The Devlin Hunter she knew was back in full force. 'You don't sound a bit surprised.'

'Considering what you put up with for me, I thought I might have a chance.' He pressed her close to him, wrapping his arms tightly with no intention of letting go.

'But you do sound relieved,' Jessica light-heartedly pointed out. She nuzzled her face into his neck. She breathed in his scent and sighed. She was home.

'I'm very relieved,' he admitted. 'I wasn't sure how I was going to make you love me. If you *could* learn to love me.'

She instinctively knew that Devlin considered himself unlovable. Jessica silently vowed to teach him otherwise. 'I've been in love with you for quite some time,' she confessed. 'But I thought my feeling were a liability, especially in an arranged marriage.'

'This may have started out as an arranged marriage,' Devlin said gruffly, 'but it is now a love marriage. We were never arranged, anyway.'

'You're right. "Arrange" makes me think of plans and smooth executions. That certainly doesn't go along with all our missteps to the altar!'

The light in his eyes dimmed at the word 'missteps'. 'I don't want you to ever regret marrying me. Or loving me.'

'I don't. Not anymore.' She cradled his face with her hands and her sapphire ring twinkled in the afternoon sun. 'I was afraid that my love for you would destroy me. I know now that's not the case.'

'I won't let that happen. We'll work on it. I want a family life that feeds you, not devours you.'

She breathed with relief. He didn't dismiss her worries. He understood. 'I'm all for that.'

'Let's start on that now,' he said and started hustling her into the house.

She dragged her feet. Jessica knew their problems were far from solved. She had no idea what he planned to do about Barry. Did he realize the full ramifications of denying his birthright? The list of questions for a moment seemed overwhelming. 'First thing first.'

'OK, anything.' Devlin flexed his knees and swooped her up into his arms.

The earth tilted under her feet. 'Devlin!' she shrieked, clinging to his shoulders.

'Oh, right. I'm supposed to warn you. Next time,' he promised.

'You bet there'll be a next time,' she said as he strode to the house. 'I want us to take a real honeymoon.' Where could they go? Somewhere no one could disturb them. A private island? A European castle? Maybe lock the gates to the vineyard and create their own private sanctuary.

'Name the place and we're there,' Devlin promised. 'Do you want a real wedding?'

She smiled at the thought of an intimate, meaningful ceremony. Right on the vineyard surrounded by everything important to them. 'Now we're talking.'

'We can discuss this later.' He kicked open the front door.

'Later?' She looked into his brown eyes blazing with desire and intense love. 'Right. Later. Much later.'

chapter twelve

One year later

Jessica tugged off a sapphire earring and switched the mobile phone to her other ear. 'No, Tracy. I can't do it.' The chauffeur-driven Rolls Royce entered the winery's main gates. The vineyard burst with life as harvest approached. Preparations for the busiest season caused a quiet buzz of activity in the air.

'Oh, come on. Please?'

'No.' She grimaced as she felt another kick. Jessica glanced down at her engorged stomach. She was bursting with life as well. Excitement flitted through her veins every time she thought about it.

'All I'm asking for is one little itty, bitty favour,' Tracy pleaded.

Rolling her eyes at her sister's words, Jessica knew that an 'itty-bitty favour' for Tracy usually required nerves of steel. 'Tracy, I understand that you're overwhelmed at the moment. I appreciate you turning to me in your hour of need. Unfortunately, I'm up to my ears in work.'

'Yeah, right.' Tracy snorted in disbelief. 'You're a lady of leisure now.'

Jessica chuckled at the label. True, she lived graciously. A well-trained domestic staff made household decisions a breeze. She delegated much of her paperwork and scheduling to her social secretary and personal assistant. Soon she would have to hire a nanny. And when she wasn't being driven around town from one appointment or social event to another, Jessica worked in her home office developing a software system for the winery's exclusive use.

Being a lady of leisure was hard work. Fun, challenging, and fulfilling, but definitely a full-time job. 'You are confusing me with Mom,' Jessica decided.

'Nah. That woman hasn't sat still since the divorce. She's making up for lost time.'

Jessica nodded in agreement. Lorraine Parks was celebrating her newfound freedom with style. Being away from Barry and their oppressive marriage had created a radical change in her mother. She was no longer scared and worried about every move. Her mother's self-confidence grew stronger with every new challenge and experience.

But not everything had changed about her mother. Lorraine still looked for someone for guidance and support. Just as Jessica had silently vowed in the hospital waiting room, she took care of her parent. That included everything from hiring a divorce lawyer to house hunting. The latter may have been a waste of time since the older woman showed no signs of allowing grass to grow under her feet.

'Doesn't she realize that taking a holiday means relaxing and enjoying the view?' Tracy mused. 'Where is she now?'

'I received a postcard from her yesterday. She's in Dubai.'

'Dubai!' Tracy shrieked. 'What is she doing there?'

'Well, it is one of the shopping capitals of the world.' Jessica made a mental note to return a call to Lorraine's financial planner who was having an apoplectic fit over the bills. She would make up the difference, knowing Devlin would insist. Devlin was extremely generous with his mother-in-law. Jessica suspected his reasons were influenced by a desire to keep Lorraine busy and out of trouble.

Tracy sighed irritably. 'I cannot believe our mother is

gallivanting around the world when my wedding is in three weeks! She is supposed to be home and acting like the mother of the bride. Doesn't she realize my wedding is this month?'

'She's aware of it. We all are,' Jessica responded dryly. 'We've been counting down the days.'

Tracy and Nicholas, Devlin's former assistant, were to be married. After watching their tempestuous affair unfold, it made Jessica wonder what exactly had occurred when Nicholas had 'detained' her twin during the sister switch.

'She's not going to be back in time,' Tracy predicted.

'Calm down.' Jessica glanced at the mansion as the Rolls coasted around the curving drive. She couldn't wait to see Devlin.

'Now, I'm really going to need your help.'

Jessica made a face at Tracy's pathetic attempt to garner her assistance. 'Don't even try that with me. You have a wedding planner, now use her. Delegate your – oh, no.' She frowned at the familiar silver Cadillac.

'What?'

'Barry is at my house.' She spotted him pacing near the front door. Jessica smiled smugly, knowing Rodgers had successfully barricaded her stepfather's attempt at bull-dozing his way into the house.

'No way! You want me to come over?' The fighting spirit threaded Tracy's voice. Some things never change, Jessica thought.

'Thanks, but no. I can handle him.' Dealing with Barry wasn't on her list of favourite things to do, but she wasn't going to shirk the responsibility.

'Are you...?'

'I'm sure,' she said firmly. Her family still thought she needed to be taken care of, to be babysat. She knew she might never be able to change their minds. Perhaps it didn't really matter. Jessica was confident she could take care of herself.

Tracy, on the other hand, was not so confident. 'If you don't call me in twenty minutes, I'm coming over.'

'No, Tracy. You have enough to do, remember? I'll talk to you later.'

'You'd better. Bye.' Her sister ended the call reluctantly.

Jessica turned off the mobile phone. What was he doing here? Since he had resumed working, Barry had made infrequent and uninvited stops at the winery. Usually it was to complain about Nicholas' executive decisions or Lorraine's alimony. The complaints were all show. A deeper reason lurked under his bluster.

Had it been anyone else, Jessica would think that Barry wanted to make excuses for seeing his son. Yet Barry never expressed any interest in a belated family reunion. There was never a glimmer of pride or fatherly affection in his eyes.

So why did he feel the need to show up at the winery? What did he want? What did he *really* want? Jessica took a deep breath and straightened her shoulders. She was going to find out, once and for all.

Devlin strode through the house with long brisk strides. His work boots left marks on the floor as each pounding step rang in the air. He vaguely noticed the staff dodging into the adjoining rooms the moment they saw his harsh expression.

The instant Rodgers rang him, Devlin's first instinct was to get Parks off his property before Jessica returned. Not only was his wife in a delicate condition, but she also couldn't abide Barry Parks. Devlin didn't want anything or anyone upsetting her.

When he heard Jessica's voice outside the front door, Devlin knew he hadn't reached Barry in time. He exhaled sharply. Now he had to figure out a way to get Jessica in the house without letting her see him physically remove Parks from their property. What was it about the Parks family that made it impossible to enjoy a tranquil early retirement?

He cocked his head as he listened to Jessica order Barry off their property. Pride enveloped him. Jessica had grown into a woman to be reckoned with. Devlin slowly opened the door so as not to interrupt her entertaining lecture on uninvited guests.

Jessica and Barry stood by the Cadillac. Devlin's gaze warmed as he saw the cool breeze playing with his wife's long brown hair. Her rosy cheeks and flashing blue eyes enhanced her pale beauty. Devlin glanced at her slender body. She vibrated with attitude. Her feet were braced and her fists rested on her hips. Jessica's pregnant stomach strained against the ocean-blue dress.

Barry sliced through her words. 'Hunter made a promise, and I'm cashing in.'

Dread wrapped around Devlin's chest. He didn't want Jessica to know about the deal he had made with the devil. Damn Parks for revealing it!

Jessica's eyes narrowed. 'I don't recall a conversation like that. You wouldn't by any chance have that in writing?'

'It was a gentlemen's agreement.'

'I see.' She paused. 'Then who sat in for you?'

A low chuckle rumbled deep in Devlin's throat. He knew Jessica was a spitfire. It was invigorating to see her act that way to Barry.

'Cut the bull. Do you know what kind of man you're married too, Jessica? He squeezed a deal out of me while I was on my deathbed.' He pressed his hand against his chest for effect. 'What kind of man would take advantage of a poor, sick, old man?'

Jessica rolled her eyes at his failed attempt for melodrama. 'A smart one, if that man was you.'

Barry sneered back at his stepdaughter. 'We made a deal. No one welches on me.' Barry thumped his fist on the roof of his car. 'No one.'

Devlin was about to launch through the doorway, but one quick look at Jessica stopped him. She didn't cower or step back. The angry action meant nothing to her.

'What exactly was the deal?' she asked. Her tone indicated that Barry was wasting her time. She clearly didn't believe a word Barry said.

Devlin winced. He knew he should have told her about the deal, even though it didn't necessarily affect their fortune. Still, he wished she wouldn't find out about it through Barry. That'd cost him!

Barry smiled like a magician about to pull a rabbit out of his hat. 'If I handed over the evidence I had on your mother, I would get a percentage of the winery.'

Jessica blinked. She looked away from her stepfather and scanned the grounds. Devlin accepted the compunction stabbing him. It had been a stupid agreement. Had it been based solely on business matters, Devlin would have rejected it outright. But their future as a couple depended on it. He had agreed to the pact, afraid of what would happen if he didn't accept the terms.

Jessica turned her attention back to her stepfather. 'But it turned out that the evidence was of no value. You shackled my mother into marriage when the proof wasn't worth the paper it was written on.' She glared at him as the old anger welled up.

Devlin's anger mirrored her own. He remembered holding the 'evidence' in his hands. It wouldn't have stood up in court, let alone Seattle's upper-class social circle. Lorraine's fear gave power to the proof, imprisoning her to years of servitude.

He and Jessica knew not to tell Lorraine the exact

weakness of Barry's evidence. They wanted to protect her from the truth. Devlin now wondered at the intelligence of that decision. Family secrets had a way of blowing up in everyone's faces.

'So what?' Barry shrugged. 'What's your point?'

'There was no evidence so, therefore, your percentage is zero,' she said. Leashed anger clipped each word.

Admiration filled Devlin. Jessica was winging it without any information to substantiate her argument. He noticed she didn't question the veracity of Barry's claim. Devlin wondered about that.

'I can manufacture evidence very easily.' Barry puffed up his chest. 'I can ruin your mother's reputation. Brand her as the criminal she is. I don't need her name or background anymore.'

Jessica clucked her tongue at the threat. 'Neither does she. Considering she's hardly in the country anymore, I don't think her reputation really matters.'

'And what about your husband's reputation?'

'What about it?' Jessica folded her arms across her chest.

Barry's eyes shifted as he studied the grounds. 'The wine industry doesn't look too kindly on a vintner who can't pay his debts.'

Jessica's face tightened with fury. 'He owes no debt to you. And this has nothing to do with the winery. You're not interested in it, no matter how much money it makes. You're interested in gaining influence over Devlin.'

'Bull. I already have influence.'

'Only in your mind,' she retorted. 'You don't have it where it matters the most. You won't have any influence over his child.'

Barry glared at Jessica. His brown eyes narrowed into slits.

'Yeah, I do know what this is about. You feel the need to

gain access and power over your grandchild.'

Devlin leaned against the doorframe and crossed his feet. It was amazing what he was discovering about his innocent wife. She understood what drove Barry, but the filth didn't dirty her view on life. Jessica was no longer naïve, but she wasn't cynical either. She was an alluring combination of optimism and realism, of girlish curiosity and womanly sophistication. Devlin knew he would enjoy the next fifty or sixty years watching this woman unfurl her full power.

'Hunter refused his inheritance,' Barry said, 'but he can't refuse it on behalf of my grandchildren.' He pointed at Jessica's stomach. 'That baby is going to be my sole heir. That gives me every right...'

'Try it and I will ruin *your* reputation,' Jessica said tersely through clenched teeth. She walked to Barry's car and opened the driver's side. 'I believe you have outstayed your welcome.'

'What?'

'You heard me. The evidence you had over Mom was worthless, but you didn't cover your tracks. While I was helping her with the paperwork for her divorce lawyer, I came upon your blackmail papers. The ones outlining how she would suffer if she didn't marry you. And what she had to suffer through during her marriage.'

Devlin's eyes widened. He didn't know about any papers. Was she trying to pull a fast one on Barry? If so, she had more chutzpah than he had assumed. If the papers were imaginary, Devlin could only applaud her plan. A plan that had obviously worked. Barry would one day realize that Jessica was an overprotective mother. She would turn into a bloodthirsty tigress if she felt her baby was in danger.

'That's...That's impossible.' Barry splayed his hands in the air. His brow furrowed as he tried to remember what he had written over a decade ago. 'Let me see them.'

'Are you kidding me?' Jessica gave him an incredulous look. 'They are locked up tight in a very safe place. I have no intentions of taking them out unless I'm forced to,' she added for emphasis.

'I don't remember any papers.' Barry stepped into his car and then halted. 'You're trying to pull one on me. It ain't going to work.'

Jessica shook her head. 'I can't believe how careless you were. But maybe that's because you knew Mom would be too scared to show them to anyone. Did you think she would feel so ashamed that she would have destroyed those papers? If you understood Mom, you would have known that she saves everything.'

'Who do you think you are, trying to blackmail me?' Barry tapped his breastbone.

'This is not blackmail,' Jessica corrected with exaggerated patience. 'I am merely explaining what the consequences will be for certain actions.'

'Don't try and get all high and mighty, you little fraud,' Barry sneered. 'Let's see how eager you are to expose me when I can expose the way you switched roles with your sister at the wedding.'

'What are you talking about?' Jessica eyes widened in a comic display of outrage. 'Did you think that was *me* going down the aisle?'

'Too right it was you. Everyone in town is still trying to figure out how you wound up as Devlin's wife. I'm sure they'll be very interested to hear the truth.'

'Barry, I can't believe you're confessing this to me.'

'What in the blazes are you talking about?' Barry looked completely lost.

'You thought you were handing Devlin the wrong bride? You knowingly took part in a fraud,' she said in a theatrical whisper.

Devlin's shoulders shook with laughter at Barry's expression. Had Devlin not seen it himself, he would never have believed that Jessica had caught Barry two-footed in the game of blackmail and deception.

'The fraud didn't occur,' Jessica continued, ignoring Barry's glowering eyes. 'But I'm sure there's some punishment for intent. I'm equally certain everyone in town would be interested in that titbit.'

His mouth tightened until it almost disappeared.

'Fortunately, the sister switch is only a figment of your imagination. One you don't have any proof to show. The paperwork showing your blackmail is a different matter,' she added with a sweet smile.

Barry sputtered. 'The statute of limitation ran out on that years ago.'

'I can always check with my lawyer on that.' She paused and gave a look of concern. 'Of course, he doesn't have the most discreet staff at hand…'

'You don't have the balls to pull that stunt,' he accused in a vicious tone.

A ferocious look melted her exaggerated expression. 'You don't mess with my family.'

'Hunter and that child are my blood. They are *my* family.'

'If your flesh and blood are so important to you, then I'm sure you'll be looking forward to their visits when you're in prison.'

Barry's flushed face turned a darker shade of red. He knew he was beaten and he couldn't stomach it. 'This isn't over,' he hissed as he sat down in his car.

'Yes, it is.' She slammed the car door shut.

Barry gunned his engine. Jessica walked backwards, closer to the house as the Cadillac swerved in reverse. The tires spun on the gravel as dust spewed into clouds. The car fishtailed for a moment before shooting towards the exit.

Devlin saw Jessica sigh and her shoulders wilt. He stepped away from the door.

'Amazing performance.'

'Devlin!' Jessica whirled around. 'I didn't see you there.'

'Neither of you did.' He strolled down the steps. 'You guys were too wrapped up in family matters.'

'Ha.' She cast a withering glare at the distant car. 'That man doesn't have an idea what family is all about.'

'You do.' He cupped her cheek with his hand. 'You handled yourself very well.'

Jessica wrinkled her nose. 'How much did you hear?'

'All of it.' He was glad he did. He knew that Jessica placed him and the baby above all else, but it was breathtaking to see her in action.

'And you didn't come to my rescue? What stopped you?' She tilted her head and looked into his eyes. Her wide smile warmed him to the bone.

'I was chomping at the bit,' Devlin admitted. The words barely described the burning tension he suffered. 'But I thought you needed to handle it.'

'Impressed you, did I?' She flipped her hair playfully and waited for the accolades to come rolling in.

'I knew you had it in you. Wasn't sure if you knew it. Do you really have Barry's blackmailing papers?'

'Yep. I consider them my "Barry insurance". Had a feeling this type of situation was going to happen. I'm surprised it took him this long to call in his markers.' A scowl marred her features. 'And what is this about you offering him a percentage of your winery?'

Devlin shrugged uncomfortably. 'It was the only way to wrestle your Mom's evidence away from him,' he admitted quietly. 'I thought I got a pretty good deal, considering.'

She linked her arms around his neck and hugged him. 'I

can't believe you almost mortgaged your dream for my mom,' she said hoarsely, as tears glistened in her blue eyes.

'For us,' Devlin corrected, looking down at her in confusion. He thought Jessica would be angry or upset. She was definitely weepy, but she looked at him like he was some knight in shining armour.

The sensation was unlike any other. A blinding white power rippled through him. He felt like he could slay any dragon or defend the castle. He could do anything for his woman. She may no longer be a damsel-in-distress, but she still needed and wanted his form of protection.

Devlin pressed her closer. He lowered his head and fused his mouth with hers. Jessica stole his breath away with a hungry kiss. His heart wanted to burst against the constricting ribcage.

Devlin bent his knees, ready to sweep Jessica into his arms. The baby fiercely kicked his belt buckle. He reared back.

'I don't think the baby likes me,' Devlin muttered, eyeing Jessica's burgeoning belly with a mix of trepidation and awe.

'We've been over this, Devlin.' Her lips tilted in a purely feminine smile. 'About the baby…'

'What?' His fingers gripped Jessica's arms.

'It's OK,' she hurriedly assured him. 'I went to the doctor's today for a check-up. They did an ultrasound.'

Devlin groaned. 'I missed it. I didn't know you were going to have it so soon.'

'Don't worry. They gave me the pictures. They're in my handbag.'

'Just tell me now.' Devlin was too impatient to look at the images. 'What is it? A boy or a girl?'

Jessica's mouth twitched. 'Well, I think the question should be "What are they?".'

His mouth sagged open. His heart slowed. His brain whirred around Jessica's words. 'Do you mean?'

'Devlin, we're going to have...' Her smile and dancing eyes beckoned him. 'Twin girls.'

epilogue

The cool October wind whistled through the trees, carrying the faint scent of autumn flowers. Grey clouds crowded the darkening sky and threatened to drizzle rain. 'One more picture with the bride and groom please,' the photographer called out.

'Can you believe it?' Nicholas stepped next to Devlin as they watched the older couple pose on the rickety bridge over the pond. 'The woman never learns. Where did she pick up this guy?'

'Majorca,' Devlin answered. He couldn't believe it either. Lorraine Parks was getting married again! Devlin was not one to believe in the superstition of 'third time's a charm', especially when Husband Number Three was significantly younger than the bride, and a well-known fortune hunter. The only good quality the slick con artist possessed was his desire to keep Lorraine happy. Devlin's monetary gift to the couple assured Husband Number Three's attentiveness would last a long time.

'This one can't be as bad as Barry.' Nicholas made the statement almost a question. The family would get rowdy if there were more than one Barry.

'He won't because we're around.' Devlin dangled the possibility of more money for his newest father-in-law if the charlatan kept out of Lorraine's financial affairs. Husband Number Three's hunger for money would make him very adaptable. Devlin's thoughtful frown turned into a scowl. 'What are you smirking at?'

Nicholas pressed his lips together as he bit back a

chuckle. 'Never imagined you holding a baby.'

'I'm getting very good at it.' He glanced down at the dark-haired infant curled against his shoulder. Rebecca had been fussy the past few minutes but now she was in her favourite spot – secure in her father's arms. She snuggled against his chest, sleepily searching for his heartbeat.

Devlin arched back slightly to accommodate his daughter while keeping an eye on Rebecca's twin. Rachel didn't allow people to hold her for long. She was too adventurous and curious. At the moment, she was raking her stubby fingers through a patch of dirt. Devlin wonder if it was an early sign of an interest in winemaking. He privately hoped he would make the winery into a worthy legacy for his children.

His children. Pride swelled inside, filling him with an everlasting strength. The two girls offered him a joy he didn't know existed. His withered heart now burst with life. Each child was special to him, yet they were very different. Very much like Jessica and Tracy.

'There's nothing easier than holding a baby,' Devlin admitted, cradling Rebecca closer and softly patting her back. You'll learn soon enough.' He tilted his head in the direction of his sister-in-law. Tracy stood in the grass with feet braced and arms akimbo. Her rounded stomach strained against a silk maternity dress.

His movement caught her eye. 'Hey, Devlin.' Tracy walked towards him. 'It was very sweet of you to host Mom's wedding at the vineyard.'

Devlin flashed a fierce glare at Tracy. He didn't like the term 'sweet', no matter how much Jessica's mother and sister described him as such. 'Don't get any ideas, Tracy. It's a one-time deal. This is a working vineyard. The last thing I need is to have a party planner trampling through my vines.'

'Aw.' She gave an exaggerated pout of her bottom lip.

'And I was hoping to have the baptismal party here.'

'No.' He would do anything for the family because it made Jessica happy and her life simpler, but he wished the in-laws would refrain from crashing in on the tranquillity of their home.

'Jessica said I could.' Tracy smiled as she pulled her trump card.

It sounded like Jessica, but Devlin decided to bluff his way through it. 'No, she didn't.'

Tracy clasped her hands behind her back like a naughty schoolgirl trying to appear innocent. 'Said we might as well get the system down pat...' She pursed her lips and looked away.

Devlin's eyes narrowed suspiciously. 'Why?'

Tracy shrugged and cheerfully refused to make eye contact. 'How should I know?'

Devlin was already scanning the yard. 'Jessica!' He grimaced as Rebecca whimpered in her sleep.

Jessica stepped away from the photographer and approached the group. 'What is it?'

He inhaled sharply at her simple beauty. The breeze mussed her hair and gave her rosy cheeks. The sheath dress was more formal than she usually wore, but it went perfectly with the sapphire earrings he had given her at the birth of the twins. Devlin thought she grew more beautiful and more fascinating each day.

'Is there something you'd like to tell me?' he asked, hoping his growl would get an immediate answer.

She slanted a deadly look at her sister. 'No, not right now.' She crouched down to brush the dirt off Rachel.

'Jessica?' His tone held a bite of warning.

She swung Rachel off the ground and onto her hip. 'I wasn't going to say anything because this is Mom's special day.'

'Spill it.'

'I'm pregnant again,' she announced, her eyes shining with pleasure.

Primal gratification seeped in Devlin's belly. 'How far along?' he asked, as Nicholas offered his Congratulations.

'Oh.' Her smile widened, dimpling her cheeks. 'Far enough to know we're going to have twins again.'

Devlin barely heard Tracy's excited squeal. The primal possession he felt for his family transmuted into something more. At one time in his life, he had strove for a moment of a just world. He had been ignorant of what life had to offer. What life with Jessica had to offer.

His gaze connected with Jessica. His surroundings grew hazy while his wife and children appeared in stark clarity. In the intimate cocoon, Devlin now knew of a world filled with passion and devotion. Of love and peacefulness. Of new beginnings and a hopeful future.

Devlin reached out and cupped Jessica's face. He stroked her cheek gently before lowering his mouth against hers. As he brushed a kiss on her soft lips, Devlin understood what it was like to reside in an ideal world, and he was convinced it would last beyond a lifetime.

Why not start a new romance today with Heartline Books. We will send you an exciting Heartline romance ABSOLUTELY FREE. You can then discover the benefits of our home delivery service: Heartline Books Direct.

Each month, before they reach the shops, you will receive four brand new titles, delivered directly to your door.

All you need to do is to fill in your details opposite – and return them to us at the address below.

Please send me my free book:

Name (IN BLOCK CAPITALS)

_____

Address (IN BLOCK CAPITALS)

_____

_____

_____

_____ Postcode _____

Freepost Address:
HEARTLINE BOOKS
PO Box 400
Swindon SN2 6EJ

We may use this information to send you offers from ourselves or
selected companies, which may be of interest to you.

If you do not wish to receive further offers
from Heartline Books, please tick this box ☐

If you do not wish to receive further offers
from other companies, please tick this box ☐

Once you receive your free book, unless we hear from you otherwise,
within fourteen days, we will be sending you four exciting new romantic
novels at a price of £3.99 each, plus £1 p&p. Thereafter, each time you
buy our books, we will send you a further pack of four titles.

You can cancel at any time! You have no obligation to ever buy a
single book.

Heartline Books –
romance at its best!

What do you think of this month's selection?

As we are determined to continue to offer you books which are up to the high standard we know you expect from Heartline, we need you to tell us about *your* reading likes and dislikes. So can we please ask you to spare a few moments to fill in the questionnaire on the following pages and send it back to us? And don't be shy – if you wish to send in a form for each title you have read this month, we'll be delighted to hear from you!

Questionnaire

Please tick the boxes to indicate your answers:

1 Did you enjoy reading this Heartline book?

Title of book: _____

A lot ☐
A little ☐
Not at all ☐

2 What did you particularly like about this book?

Believable characters ☐
Easy to read ☐
Enjoyable locations ☐
Interesting story ☐
Good value for money ☐
Favourite author ☐
Modern setting ☐

3 If you didn't like this book, can you please tell us why?

_____

_____

4 Would you buy more Heartline Books each month if they were available?

Yes ☐

No – four is enough ☐

5 What other kinds of books do you enjoy reading?

Historical fiction ☐
Puzzle books ☐
Crime/Detective fiction ☐
Non-fiction ☐
Cookery books ☐

Other _____

_____

6 Which magazines and/or newspapers do you read regularly?

a) _____

b) _____

c) _____

d) _____

And now a bit about you:

Name _____

Address _____

_____

_____ Postcode _____

Thank you so much for completing this questionnaire.
Now just tear it out and send it in an envelope to:

HEARTLINE BOOKS
PO Box 400
Swindon SN2 6EJ

(and if you don't want to spoil this book, please feel free
to write to us at the above address with your comments
and opinions.)

Ref: TWB

Have you missed any of the following books:

The Windrush Affairs *by Maxine Barry*
Soul Whispers *by Julia Wild*
Beguiled *by Kay Gregory*
Red Hot Lover *by Lucy Merritt*
Stay Very Close *by Angela Drake*
Jack of Hearts *by Emma Carter*
Destiny's Echo *by Julie Garrett*
The Truth Game *by Margaret Callaghan*
His Brother's Keeper *by Kathryn Bellamy*
Never Say Goodbye *by Clare Tyler*
Fire Storm *by Patricia Wilson*
Altered Images *by Maxine Barry*
Second Time Around *by June Ann Monks*
Running for Cover *by Harriet Wilson*
Yesterday's Man *by Natalie Fox*
Moth to the Flame *by Maxine Barry*
Dark Obsession *by Lisa Andrews*
Once Bitten...Twice Shy *by Sue Dukes*
Shadows of the Past *by Elizabeth Forsyth*
Perfect Partners *by Emma Carter*
Melting the Iceman *by Maxine Barry*
Marrying A Stranger *by Sophie Jaye*
Secrets *by Julia Wild*
Special Delivery *by June Ann Monks*
Bittersweet Memories *by Carole Somerville*
Hidden Dreams *by Jean Drew*
The Peacock House *by Clare Tyler*
Crescendo *by Patricia Wilson*

Complete your collection by ringing the Heartline Hotline on 0845 6000504, visiting our website <u>www.heartlinebooks.com</u> or writing to us at Heartline Books, PO Box 400, Swindon SN2 6EJ